ACTION SHOT

LOVE, CAMERA, ACTION #2

ELISE FABER

SNARKY BOOKS FOR SNARKY MINDS

ACTION SHOT
BY ELISE FABER

ACTION SHOT
Copyright © 2020 Elise Faber
Print ISBN-13: 978-1-63749-013-6
Ebook ISBN-13: 978-1-946140-55-5
Cover Art by Jena Brignola

LOVE, CAMERA, ACTION

Dotted Line

Action Shot

Close Up

End Scene

ONE

Artemis, Five Years Before

HE DIDN'T KNOW I was a woman.

That was wont to happen with a name like—

"Artie?"

I didn't hold it against the young male director for staring around the room—devoid of people except for the two of us—in confusion for several long moments. With a name like Artie, I was often confused for a man. Especially considering that I was in the movie business, and specifically production, which was a male-dominated field.

Though I had to give it to him, he recovered quickly.

His smile was charming, his looks even more so, but . . . I was going to give him bad news.

I couldn't stand his films.

Any of them.

He was talented, an up-and-coming young director who could barely grow a beard, but he had vision, he was smart, and he could shoot a movie.

They just weren't for me.

And so, I was going to pass on this project.

Probably stupid, considering he was going to be the next hot thing in Hollywood, but also . . . that was me—not the stupid part, but the going with my heart and gut and *never* working on a film that I wasn't passionate about.

I'd promised myself that before getting back into the industry, after spending way too much of my childhood in the limelight, and I'd kept that promise for the last sixteen years.

My films showcased women in strong, fulfilling roles. They featured talented female comedians and people of all colors, genders, and sexual orientations.

I made films that weren't Hollywood. Insert the air quotes here. But it was true. They *weren't* what Hollywood typically made—huge budgets, lots of action and explosions. Not that there was anything wrong with those movies. I loved a good shoot-em-up.

But I wasn't passionate about making them.

It wasn't pandering, me producing these kinds of films. Audiences understood when they were being played.

They also understood genuine.

I'd built my career on that notion, and I'd become successful. But it had taken a solid ten years of working and hustling— and did I mention *hustling*—before I'd become well-known enough for producing and not simply being part of a infamous family and that I'd actually made some money.

And also four Oscars, but I didn't need to brag.

Snorting to myself, I lifted my brows and raised my glass to my lips.

"You're Artie." Pierce Daniels, the aforementioned handsome, young director, answered his own question and sat in the chair opposite me.

It was late-afternoon in L.A., the restaurant we were in was one of my favorites, and I'd become fancy and important enough

—*ha*—that they'd let me come in before they opened. Fancy and important had its perks, though this particular perk was mostly because I liked the chef—female, insanely good with all things carb-related (which was a feat sometimes in the land of Hollywood), and driven—and so I'd become a silent partner in the restaurant.

"I'm Artie," I confirmed. "Nice to meet you, Pierce."

He pulled out a laptop and I laughed internally. God, I loved energetic new blood, loved he was so excited about this project that he'd brought materials to go over. I'd been in the industry long enough to be jaded and cynical.

Pierce had exactly the kind of enthusiasm we needed in this town.

"Thanks for meeting with me," he said, powering up the computer. "I loved *In For a Penny*"—the first film I'd produced that had made its way to the awards circuit and also had garnered me my first Oscar—"but I think my favorite is actually *Into the Fire*."

I smiled. "Thanks for saying that." I set my glass on the table. "I was able to screen your most recent film. It's going to be a hit."

Notice I didn't subscribe to false flattery.

Objectively, I didn't like his movies.

However, that didn't mean I was immune to the knowledge that he was supremely talented.

He froze for a minute, studying me closely, and I was locked in place by a pair of the prettiest eyes I'd ever seen. Stormy gray with indigo bisecting their depths. Those irises darkened, understanding clouding his expression.

Click.

The laptop shut.

"It's a no," he announced, sitting back in his chair almost haphazardly.

I frowned.

"You're a no on the film."

My fingers circled the stem of my water glass. "It's a no," I agreed. "Probably the stupidest no I'll ever give, considering how successful you'll be in the next year or two." I lifted the cup to my lips, took a sip. "But the script just isn't something I'll ever make."

A lock of brown hair drifted over his forehead, giving the twenty-something-year-old director the appearance of someone even younger.

He brushed it back, almost annoyingly.

"Why not?" he asked. "The female lead is strong, more powerful than most of the men in the film, and that dynamic is something you specialize in."

Cute.

"Yes, she *is* strong." I waited a beat. "However, that strength is undermined by a theme of the male co-star saving the day every step of the way. I counted at least three fight scenes where she's nearly beaten before the hero sweeps in to rescue her, not to mention his masterful ability to always get her naked and the snarky comments he makes about her driving skills."

Pierce was quiet for a long time. Then he nodded. "You're right."

The waiter came over and set a plate in front of me then handed a menu to Pierce. He took it, ordering an iced tea.

"You don't have to stay, if you don't want," I told him. "But if you do, I'll still buy you lunch."

His brows pulled down. "I thought I was buying *you* lunch."

A shake of my head. "I usually pay if I'm delivering disappointing news."

He laughed. "Ah. The stories of you are true."

I'd been busily spearing a forkful of handmade pasta,

readying to shove it in my mouth, when he spoke. "What the hell does that mean?" I asked, after chewing and swallowing.

"Just that everyone says you're the most honest person in Hollywood."

Shrugging, I stuck the fork in my mouth and moaned when the delicious brown butter sauce made every single one of my taste buds orgasm. "It's true," I agreed.

He tilted his head to the side, considering. "So, what did you think of *Sunday Night*?"

"Hated it."

He burst into laughter and set the menu on the table, gesturing to the waiter. "I'll have what she's having." The waiter nodded and Pierce turned back to face me. "How about *Blue*?

"Nope. Didn't like it."

One brown brow rose. "Well, it's better than hate, so I'll take it. Though, I'm almost afraid to ask what you think of *Life and—*"

"Worst one of the bunch."

More laughter as he grabbed his laptop off the table and stuck it into his backpack. "I do love an honest woman."

It was my turn to lift a brow. "What's that right there?" I waved my hand at his chest. "What's going on with all of that?"

"With what?" he asked innocently.

"This smolder nonsense you have going on."

His lips twitched. "Smolder?"

"Don't tell me you're one of those guys who's too good for Disney movies," I said and shoved another bite into my mouth. "*Tangled* is the best of the bunch."

"That's the crazy talking," he countered. "Clearly *The Emperor's New Groove* is better."

I gasped. "Them's fighting words, Pierce Daniels." But my lips twitched. "Pull the lever?" I asked innocently, quoting one of my favorite lines from the film.

Heat flickered in his eyes and head leaned forward. "Wrong lever?"

I laughed. "Okay, so maybe you do have some Disney street cred."

"Actually," he said, leaning back slightly to allow the waiter to set the plate in front of him. "I think those two things are actually mutually exclusive." A beat. "But thanks for appreciating it. Even *if* that's the only thing you appreciate about me."

"That is true," I teased, shoving a bite of pasta into my mouth and barely able to hold back my moan of pleasure.

Pierce gave me an affronted look, but then he picked up a forkful of food and stuck it in his mouth.

I waited.

His eyes widened in surprise.

I knew the feeling because I'd experienced it just over a year ago, when I'd first tasted the chef's food. Hence, my being a silent partner in a risky investment. Still, good food was half the battle and I'd eaten here enough to know that the other important part—service—was also exceptional.

But Pierce didn't know that.

"This is delicious," he said around the bite, which meant it sounded a lot like "Shish sish shulishush."

"Is this where I say chew with your mouth closed before surrendering to the smolder?"

He wiped his mouth with a napkin, set down the fork. "This is where I say I don't give two shits about anything besides the amazing food on my plate." He dropped the napkin back into his lap. "How did you find this place?"

I shrugged. "A lady doesn't give away her secrets."

Stormy gray-blue eyes went hot. "I bet I can convince you."

My pussy clenched. Straight up, right then. With a single look. *Uh-oh.* "I don't date children."

He laughed. "I'm twenty-two. That's hardly a child."

"Pierce. I'm thirty-seven."

"So?"

He meant it, too, I could tell.

"So, I don't date people who work with me."

His laughter burned a hole straight down to my middle. "I think we've quite established the fact that we're not going to be working together."

He had a point. And the stink knew it, given the way those hot eyes traced me up and down.

"Eat your pasta," he ordered huskily. Normally orders from men pissed me off, especially men who were many years younger than me, who deigned to think they had a right to give me orders, but there was something about Pierce's gaze, heavy with approval and desire, that made it less annoying and more . . . promising.

I lifted a brow. "And if I don't?"

"I'll just have to—" He broke off and waggled his brows, making like he was going to grab my plate.

I lifted my fork threateningly.

He laughed, went back to his own entrée. "Thanks for lunch."

My carefully constructed bite of pasta fell onto my plate. "I thought we'd established *you* were paying," I said and when he did nothing more but chuckle and then smolder at me again, before continuing to devour his lunch, I knew I was in trouble.

Then deep shit when he snagged the waiter and handed him his card.

And then falling down into a crevice of even deeper shit when he gently tugged my ponytail out from underneath the collar of my jacket when I slipped it on.

Between the table and front door, I considered my options.

At the front door, I made a decision.

I took his hand and pulled him over to my car.

TWO

Pierce

ARTEMIS WAS the most beautiful woman I'd ever seen.

Hands down. No comparison.

Eyes the color of the Pacific, hair the color of honey. A body that was more incredible than I could have ever dreamed of—hips and ass and breasts and—

Her fingers went to her shirt, slowly tugging at the length of silk that was wrapped around her throat. The pale pink made a quiet swooshing sound as the silk slid free, and my cock twitched. I'd been dreaming about doing that the entire lunch, pulling the fabric to the side, exposing the skin underneath. I'd bet she would taste like sunshine. Or maybe sweet like honey. Or spicy like the fire she'd dished out over pasta.

When her fingers went to the top button on her blouse, I stepped close and halted her movements, taking her hands into mine. I didn't want to look a gift horse in the mouth, but I also wasn't the kind of guy to take advantage.

Gently, I brought her hands to my chest, opened my mouth—

She slipped free of my grip, rose on tiptoe, and laid a finger across my lips. "Save the noble speech for some other girl," she said. "I wouldn't have brought you back to my house if I wasn't sure. But *I* should ask *you* if you're sure you want to do this." She tapped my lips lightly. "It doesn't matter how many orgasms you give me, I'm still not going to help you make that movie."

I smiled. I *liked* this woman. We'd known each other for all of an hour, and I already felt as though I'd known her my whole life.

Especially when she added, "I wouldn't want to use my very powerful position and—"

I nipped her fingers, and she jerked her hand back. "That was a very naughty thing to do young Pierce—"

One movement and I'd tugged her against me. "Is that what this is?"

"*What* is?" she asked, burying her nose in my throat.

"You have some cougar fantasy?" I teased. "Not that I'm opposed. For an old chick, you're hot—"

She gasped, outrage invading her expression.

Which gave me the perfect opportunity to drop my mouth to hers, to slip my tongue past her lips, and tease—

She bit me.

"Fuck," I grunted, pulling back.

"I'm hot for an *old chick*?"

My smile escaped, even though I tried to keep it in. "Yup. That exactly."

Her palm slid down my chest, nails digging in, moving lower. I'd appreciated the bright red nails over lunch, watching the flash of crimson appear as she ate, but I didn't think I was going to enjoy those cherry tips repeating the action beneath my pants, so I caught her hands, pinned them in one of mine. "You know I'm teasing."

"*Old chick?*" she asked again.

"I'm. Teasing."

"Out." She pointed to the front door.

Oh shit. I'd seriously fucked up. My heart sank as I scrambled to come up with a way to salvage this situation. If I didn't, I might end up with permanent blue balls. "Artemis—"

Her eyes narrowed. "Artie."

"Artie," I repeated hurriedly. "I didn't mean—" I froze, head cocking to the side. Had her lips just twitched? Fucking hell, they *had*. The little stink. Deciding to give it just as good as she was, I reached up and tied the strip of silk back around her neck. "I'll just go then," I said, hanging my head.

Her eyes widened. "I—"

Nope. Two could play these games.

"I shouldn't have said that." I shook my head, dropping my gaze to my feet so she wouldn't see me fighting a smile. "It was totally—"

"Oh my God." She stomped one heel-clad foot. "You're totally fucking with me."

My eyes darted up, clashing with the bright blue of hers. "Yes." A beat. "I'd rather be fucking *you*, though." I slid my arm around her waist, fingers slipping just underneath the hem of her shirt. "If that's something you're still interested in."

"The fucking *me*? Or the fucking with each other?"

I nipped her throat. "The first."

"Interested," she murmured. "But this can only be for one night."

I paused, not sure I'd be willing to settle for just a single night with the most interesting woman I'd ever met.

She pulled back, glanced up into my eyes. "Deal?"

"Deal." I'd worry about the one-time thing later.

A smile curved my lips as I reached for the top button on her blouse, flicking it open to reveal a tempting triangle of pale flesh. Dropping my head, I pressed a kiss there then dropped my fingers to the next, slipping it through the buttonhole. Another kiss to silken skin before moving through the rest, peeling the pale pink silk wide open to reveal a soft stomach and a nude bra.

Not lace, not particularly revealing.

Still containing the hottest set of tits I'd ever seen.

I fell to my knees, darted my tongue out to taste her belly button, letting it drift up to tease the sensitive skin just beneath her breasts. Which was the point she let her arms fall, the shirt dropping from her shoulders to tangle around her wrists.

Perfect.

I gripped those wrists, holding them captive then used my other hand to nudge up her bra and suck one pink nipple into my mouth. Sweet like honey. Spicy like pepper. The sunshine was absent, mostly because I had absolutely no clue as to what it actually tasted like.

Artie jerked when my lips hit that tight little bud, flexing against my grip before pushing herself closer. "More," she groaned.

I preferred to *give* direction, but I could damn well take it in this situation.

Releasing her arms and yanking the shirt off, I continued working that sensitive nub, pulling on it deeply, using my tongue and teeth, learning what she preferred, what made her cry out, what made her squirm against me.

"Enough," she said, trying to pull back, but I simply swept her up into my arms, walking down the hall as I slammed my mouth down onto hers.

As far as first kisses went, it was out of order, tasting her mouth after her breasts, but damn if I was going to regret having her nipples on my tongue. Still, I'd been intending on finding a horizontal surface as quickly as possible, but her lips meeting mine, her tongue and teeth meeting me stroke for stroke and nip for nip, froze me in place.

Or rather, it had me twisting and pinning her against the wall, shoving myself between her legs as she spread them wide, grinding my cock against her center.

She yanked at my shirt, fumbling with the buttons.

Distantly, I heard a few *plinks* as the round plastic circles hit the hardwood floor, but I couldn't summon the energy to care that Artie had probably just ruined the one nice shirt I owned. Yes, I'd directed a few films, two of which were considered box office successes, but the pay from them had been shit.

Though, I'd recently been offered a few new jobs with good paychecks.

The money just hadn't hit my account as of yet.

But Artie didn't care about my one good shirt or my paycheck, she was scrabbling at the material covering my chest, and the sexy mewling noises she was making in the back of her throat had my cock twitching.

Control.

But also . . . I needed to be inside her.

Eventually, I used my hips to pin her firmly against the wall so I could tear off my shirt and toss it to the floor.

"Fucking finally," she murmured, running her hands over the planes of my chest, almost reverently. At least until she slightly dug her nails in, making heat burst out from my chest, arrowing straight to my groin and making my head spin. "Mouth. Now."

She didn't say where, and I had my own plans.

I took her lips in a kiss that had us both groaning and arching against each other, her legs convulsing, her hips tilting and gyrating. I ground against her, eventually breaking for air, but using the opportunity to kiss my way along her jaw, down her throat, nipping at her collarbones. Gently, I lowered her legs to the ground, making sure she was steady on her heels before kneeling and reaching for the button on her slacks.

Her hands stopped mine.

"No?" I asked.

"Hell, yes," she murmured. "But these heels aren't exactly for standing. Help me take them off?"

I was torn between asking why the hell she was wearing shoes that weren't adequate for standing and shrugging off the intricacies of the feminine mind so I could get my mouth on her pussy.

I took option two, lifting one foot then the other and tugging off her shoes.

This time when I returned to the button on her slacks, she didn't stop me, just arched her back slightly and shimmied her hips so the material fell to the floor.

My mouth went dry.

Lace. It didn't match the bra, but the turquoise was skimpy and see-through, and the glimpse I got of her pussy through the flimsy fabric was enough to have white edging my vision.

I had to get my tongue in there.

One swift movement had the underwear at her ankles, another and it went sailing in the direction of her heels.

Artie didn't shy, didn't hesitate. She just spread her thighs and gave me pink, glistening folds.

White haze turned red, and I dove at her.

THREE

Artie

YOUTH HAD ITS PERKS.

Boundless energy, eager tongues, fingers that—

Pierce pressed the flat of his tongue to my clit, and I about shot out of my skin, but by the time I'd opened my mouth to tell him to go easy, he'd already gentled his strokes, slowing down and coaxing me back up, edging me toward a peak I knew would be the most intense I'd ever experienced.

Slow and steady. Then fast and hard. Teasing then almost too much. And yet I was spiraling up, progressively climbing that precipice.

One finger teased my entrance, circling and gently probing then sliding up to stroke just beneath my clit. It was the most coordinated—and pleasurable—experience of my life, having every bit of Pierce's focus directed at me.

I saw the director in him, the way he was able to reduce the world down to a single focal point, capturing my reactions, putting them together with his actions to create something that was intense and fulfilling, and . . . the best fucking sexual experience of my life.

That teasing finger slipped back down, but instead of teasing, it slid home. The abrupt invasion made me cry out, my hips arching forward—

Right into Pierce's mouth.

He sucked my clit, worked his finger, and . . .

I exploded.

Pleasure spiraled out of my center and tore through my limbs, sparking flames through my nerves, making my mind haze over, my knees go weak. And he kept working me, wringing every drop of pleasure out of me until I was a limp mess cuddling against his chest, both of us collapsed on the hardwood floor.

We hadn't made it ten steps from the front door.

That had to be a fucking record.

Fucking record.

Heh.

My lips twitched, and Pierce brushed my hair out of my face. "What is it?" he asked softly. "What's put that look on your face?" One brow came up suggestively. "I'm hoping it's because you just experienced the best orgasm of your life?"

I chuckled. "I'll tell you some other time."

"So, it's not my orgasms?" His face fell, but I was wise to his tricks by now.

I lightly smacked his chest. "Yes, the orgasm was a good one, you big faker." I tapped my chin, considering. "In the top hundred, for sure."

He snorted, poked me in the ribs—

With his finger.

Heh.

Orgasm-drunk, but that wasn't a bad problem to have. I giggled, both at my joke and then because he was tickling me.

"You're drunk," he accused, fingers dancing over my hip.

"I had one cocktail at lunch," I teased. "It takes more than that to get an *old chick* drunk."

"It was a joke," he muttered and amended. "How about pleasure-drunk?"

"I was thinking orgasm-drunk," I said with another giggle, but then he was kissing me and my laughter faded, thighs clenching instead as pleasure began slowly curling in my center. The man could fucking kiss.

"Bedroom?" He broke away to ask, scooping me up effortlessly at the same time.

Twenty-fucking-two.

Holy shit.

I could work with this.

Pointing down the hall, I said, "Last door on the right," and then I made myself useful, running my tongue up his throat, sucking lightly, then kissing my way across his jaw.

His mouth teased mine, coming close, drifting away, but by the time we made it through the door to my bedroom, we weren't interested in teasing.

The heat in his eyes matched the fire burning through me.

Pierce dropped me to the mattress, and I scrambled up, yanking open my bedside drawer to extract a condom and toss it next to the pillow. He was working on the button of his slacks, drawing down the zipper, pushing the fabric down and tossing it to the floor.

Black boxer briefs.

Yup, that was exactly right.

Especially when they were the punctuation mark on the most incredible set of abs I'd ever laid eyes on.

"Twenty-two," I murmured, stroking a finger between the indentions. "Yes. Thank you, universe."

He snorted. "It's the not-having-enough-to-eat diet."

My brows drew down, heart sinking. "What? You don't—"

"Starving artist is a term for a reason, Artie," he said lightly. "But I'm not starving anymore, if that's what you're worried about. In fact, I'll be sporting a beer belly in no time." He nipped her ear. "I was joking. I'm fine."

I forced a smile. I wasn't generally a soft mark, but I definitely didn't like the idea of this funny, kind man not having enough to eat. "If you—"

He cut my words off with a kiss. "I'm fine." A flick of his tongue. "Now, can we regain some focus? I don't think that discussing my diet is all that sexy."

"It gave you these abs," I said, ignoring the twinge of emotion. "So, I find I can't hate it."

He laughed, tugged me so I was sprawled beneath him. "Now, where were we?"

"I think you were putting that sharp tongue to use."

"I think *you* mean highly skilled."

"I don't care what you call it," I declared, "so long as you get it in my mouth."

A wicked grin. "I can do that."

Then his tongue was in my mouth and there were no more words, just caresses and kisses and moans. He kissed me until I forgot all about starving artists and the real world. He kissed me until I was a writhing mess that could barely remember my own name.

He kissed me until my hands stopped stroking his chest and drifted south, slipping under the waistband of his boxer briefs to cup the hard length of him.

Groaning, he pumped into my hand, not protesting when I reached for the condom and rolled it on, not delaying when I lay back and spread my thighs, not hesitating to thrust deep and—

"Holy fucking shit," I moaned.

"Fuck, yes," he groaned.

Pure chemistry, or perhaps it was just that our personalities melded, *though* I couldn't deny that he was really fucking hot—but whatever the reason, the feel of him sliding home, of filling me to the brim, had surpassed his mouth as the singular most pleasurable experience of my life.

He didn't fuck like a twenty-two-year-old—fast and furious and single-minded.

He was intense, yes, but he was also calculating.

Deducing my pleasure down to precise movements, using deliberate touches and strokes, the man played my body better than *anyone* I'd ever been with. And I'd been with a whole variety—young, old, shy, arrogant, black, white, Asian. My work brought me all over the world, and I wasn't a prude. If there was chemistry and I liked the man, and if he was into me in return, I went for it.

But Pierce was the best I'd ever gone for.

I was almost disappointed we would only be together this one time, that I would only ever allow myself one time with him.

Then I focused on how lucky I was to have this moment with Pierce.

Maybe I worked best in temporaries, but that didn't mean I couldn't enjoy it for all it was worth.

"Hey." A nip to my jaw, his hips slowing to a halt. "Where'd you go?"

I smiled up at him. "You're doing great"—he snorted—"it's my brain that doesn't like to cooperate."

"Hmm." He dropped his head, so his mouth was very near my ear. "How about we do something to get that brain of yours to stop messing up what I happen to think was a pretty incredible . . ."

Hands weaving into his hair, I brought his lips to mine. "Fucking," I murmured when we broke apart for air, thoughts fading, hips already moving against him. "Yes, it's good. Yes, I'm into it. No, my brain never shuts the hell up."

"As a person with a similarly annoying brain that can't keep quiet"—Pierce darted out his tongue, tasting the corner of my mouth—"I have an idea about how to fix that."

My lips curved. "I think I'm going to like it."

A smirk. "I think you are."

And then, true to his word, he took my mind off my thoughts. Mouth dropping to mine, he braced himself with one hand and slid the other down. He moved, thrusting deep, fingers delving between my thighs to circle my clit. Just like before, his focus was intense and perfect and because of him, for the first time in forever, my brain went completely clear of extraneous blips of reason. It was able to focus solely on him, on us, on what I was feeling.

Uh-oh.

But even *I* was too far gone to recognize that warning.

Instead, I wrapped my legs around Pierce's hips, tilted my pelvis to allow his fingers better access to my clit, and held on as he rode me straight over the edge to orgasm.

Yup, I thought after my pleasure had faded and thoughts began invading my brain again, *best fuck ever.*

FOUR

Pierce, Five Years Later

I SPOTTED her on the red carpet.

Blonde hair cascading down her spine—and I said spine because her dress was completely backless, giving me glimpses of bare skin and a backbone I'd kissed my way down five years before.

One incredible night half a decade ago.

And I could still recall every touch, every moan, every moment.

I sucked in a breath, shifted from foot to foot, trying to force those memories down. Most of the time I was fine. My work kept me busy and it wasn't like I'd gone full-monk after we'd had our fun.

But Artemis Miller had left her mark on me.

Now every time I saw her, I could remember how she felt as she wrapped her thighs around my hips, how she kissed, how—

"Pierce!" She waved an arm and hurried over, somehow navigating the carpet and long train of her dress in five-inch heels without issue.

I caught her arm when she came close enough, bending to press a kiss to each of her cheeks in turn. "How are you?"

"Great. Great," she said. "But what about you?" She cupped my jaw. "You look incredible! I heard you were filming in Hawaii. Is this"—she dropped her hand from my face and gestured at my body from toe to forehead—"tan from work or play?" A wink. "I'm guessing play."

"It's—"

"Pierce, Artie, give us a look!" a photographer shouted.

Obediently, we both spun to face the crowd of lenses. I definitely didn't love the sea of black circles staring down at me— hence the reason I spent most of my time *behind* the camera— while Artie never seemed to be fazed by anything.

She allowed the paparazzi a few shots in a couple of different poses then linked her arm with mine and led us off the marks.

Her raised eyebrow had me answering her previously interrupted question. "It's mostly work, though I did get in three days of surfing after we wrapped."

"You're going to get eaten by a shark one day, you know that, right?"

"Meh," I teased back in what had become a familiar conversation over the last years of running into each other at events like this. "I'm more likely to die in my car on the way home from surfing than from a shark."

"With the way you drive?" She sniffed. "That's probably true."

"Hey! I've been in a car with *you* driving," I teased. "I seemed to remember very desperately clinging to the Oh Shit handle."

"Lies!"

We both laughed and I felt the same pang I always experienced when I ran into Artie at industry affairs. Longing. Bittersweet. Same as I'd felt when I'd woken the next morning in her bed to find her gone, a note on the nightstand thanking me for a great night and telling me to take my time in her shower and fill my stomach from her fridge because she'd flown halfway around the world for her latest project.

One night.

Hadn't been enough.

And for all my plans of dealing with it later, I could hardly be congratulated for my skills. Artie had handled me, effortlessly and wonderfully, while at the same time insinuating an impenetrable barrier between us.

Distance and aplomb.

She had it in spades.

"How's your latest?" I asked, keeping our arms linked as we started to stroll through the open doors that would lead into the theater where the award show would be held.

Her lips curved, excitement filling her pretty blue eyes. "It's going great. We're actually ahead of schedule and our lead"— she named an up-and-coming Asian comedian—"is just exceeding every expectation. We'd hoped she would be able to pull off the dramatic role, but I can't lie and say I wasn't the teeniest bit worried."

"Teeniest bit?"

She blew out a breath, pale pink lips forming a very distracting O that had my cock remembering that mouth very intimately and forcing me to lock down the memories of our night together. "Technical terms, I know." A laugh. "What's happening after Hawaii?"

I'd just finished filming the remake of a famous comic book big budget movie. "Not much," I admitted. "I'm going to be bogged down in post-production for a while, but I don't actually have my next project lined up."

Her brows raised. "I can't believe you haven't had offers."

I shook my head. "I've had offers." Loads of them, but none of them were *mine* either. Not like when I'd first been on the scene and passionate project ideas were burning holes in my back pockets.

Now, I was being offered someone else's ideas. Which was great.

Those ideas were the reason I had a big bank balance and two houses. But they weren't mine and while I enjoyed working on them, felt a connection to the work and process—I wouldn't have worked on them if I didn't—those ideas still . . . well, they fell a little flat.

I wanted something that was mine.

Like the old days.

I smiled and patted Artie's hand. She'd probably get a kick out of me lamenting the good old days that were all of a whole five or six years ago.

But I also knew she'd get it.

"I'm fine. Just haven't found that Cinderella yet."

It was a credit to the connection we had that she didn't miss what I was getting at, or question my decision to randomly bring the famed princess into our conversation.

"No glass slipper projects," she murmured with a nod. "Hmm. I actually have something I think—"

"Pierce!"

We turned to see Bill, one of my executive producers on the remake project, waving us down. I glanced down at Artie, but she was already releasing my arm. "Go," she murmured. "I bet that entertainment show wants to get an interview."

"I'll see you late—"

Bill clapped his hand down on my shoulder, nodding at Artie briefly. "I was just talking with Andre over at the network and . . ."

And socializing time was over.

I stopped by Andre to discuss some quick marketing issues then gave a soundbite to the entertainment show that Artie had mentioned. Then I was pulled aside by my lead actor in the film I was promoting that day and asked my opinion on acceptance speeches he'd had written for him.

Probably presumptive, but I supposed being prepared was better than "umming" and "uhhing" on stage.

Then I gave a few more interviews, took a few more pictures, and finally, *finally* made it into the theater. Initially, I'd loved all the hoopla that came with having been part of a film that was popular enough to warrant award nods. Now, I understood it was part of the process and did what I needed to do. But realistically, all I wanted to do was get the night over with so I could go home and have pizza delivered.

Because anyone who was anyone didn't come to the carpet early.

Which meant that anyone who was anyone also didn't get a chance to eat.

Plenty of booze though.

Sometimes that worked out for those on the receiving end of awards with spectacular results and sometimes . . . with spectacular failures.

Snorting to myself, I walked over to the bar and ordered a club soda, not planning on being one of those award receivers who went viral for all the wrong reasons. Not that I realistically thought I'd be on stage that evening. The other directors' films were much better and had critical acclaim. Mine was popular and had made a shit-ton of money, but it was a black sheep among typical Hollywood nominees.

See?

I could evaluate myself realistically.

And I was fine with making movies that made people

happy, that entertained and provided some escapism . . . even if that meant I didn't get to take home a gilded trophy.

I just needed to find my—*fuck*, but I was going to think it— because I just needed to find *my* happy again.

I—

Was spinning.

Sighing, I forced the thoughts out of my mind, finished my club soda, then went to make my rounds. I did my job. I schmoozed and shook hands and networked and laughed. Then I sat and looked dutifully on, clapping for a winner that wasn't me. Which was fine. I was alone, but I was where I had always dreamed I would be. I'd find what was missing, or I'd realize I wasn't actually missing anything at all.

There. Done. Get over it.

But as I went about my night, I couldn't help but watch Artie as she went about hers, smiling and laughing and gener- ally charming everyone she spoke to.

She made it look absolutely effortless.

Still, I wondered if she felt the same emptiness inside her that I did.

And *if* she did, then did the careful distance she kept between herself and the rest of the world make the emptiness easier to bear?

MUCH LATER THAT EVENING, I was chowing down on my pizza when there was a knock at my door. Slice in hand, I got up from the couch and made my way over, glancing through the peephole to see a harried-looking girl standing outside, clutching a bag to her chest.

I unlocked it, tugged it open. "Can I help you?"

"My boss told me to deliver this to you."

I didn't take the bag she extended. "Who's your boss?"

"Artie Mil—"

My fingers found the handle before she finished the name, peeking inside to see an envelope with Artie's handwriting on it. Heart skipping a beat, I turned my attention back to the girl in front of me. "You have a ride home?"

She nodded. "I drove."

"Okay."

Her feet stayed firmly planted on my porch.

"Did you need something else?"

She blinked. "Oh. Um. Nope." Spinning, she hustled down the steps and out to the street. I waited until she was in her car and driving away before I went back inside.

The envelope smelled like Artie.

Or maybe I was just hallucinating.

Either way, I opened it up and read. It didn't take long because there were only two words.

For inspiration.

-A

Curved, hurried strokes, exactly like the note I'd kept from five years before. And yes, I was critically aware of how pathetic that made me, not that it was going to stop me from keeping this one as well.

Gently, I folded and pocketed the paper then looked into the bag.

A book.

I sucked in a breath—in disappointment, in anticipation? In that moment, I couldn't be sure. The only thing I *was* sure about was sitting back down on the couch, grabbing another slice, and cracking open the book and beginning to read.

I was hooked before finishing the first page.

FIVE

Artie

MY CELL RANG JUST as I stepped out of my car.

I'd taken a red-eye to Iceland right after the awards ceremony in order to approve a few shooting locations my field producer had scouted out.

Already, I was in love, even while understanding that filming here was going to be difficult with our schedule. The project was slotted to begin shooting in October, which meant we had a narrow window in which to get the necessary shots in the right light and weather conditions.

Still, the pictures I'd received from the field producer and director had almost convinced me, despite the risks to schedule.

The drive from the airport and my current stopover had done the rest.

We'd film here and figure the rest out later.

Sighing in satisfaction, I lifted my cell to my ear and said, "Hello?" Besides, the weather in October was supposed to be some of the best and—

"Does this mean you'll finally work with me?"

My lips pulled into a smile. "Pierce."

"I didn't get any sleep last night, thanks to you," he murmured, and I tried, quite desperately, though I would take that admission to my grave, to hold back a shiver at his voice. I'd heard it with alarming frequency over the last years, the slight bedroom rasp that he never used in public.

Just to me.

Just in my bed.

"Does that mean you like it?" I asked, trying to focus.

"It's fucking *everything*."

I laughed. "I never understand why people say that. It's just a book. Yes, it's a story I thought you might like, and"—I smiled at the driver and walked a few feet further from the car, lifting my DSLR to snap a few shots of the landscape—"it can't put food on the table or cure cancer or whatever *everything* encompasses."

"It's *everything* when it makes my heart sing with joy," he murmured. "Or my fingers itch for my camera or for my laptop to frantically type up ideas. It's everything when I close my eyes and see nothing but the shots I'll use to tell this story."

My breath caught, words failing me for several heartbeats. "I'm glad you like it."

His voice slid down my spine. "I more than like it, I *love* it."

He loved it. I smiled, repositioning the camera and taking a few shots that weren't the pretty landscape, but instead encompassed the logistics area. Where we'd house the crew, where the actors might stay between takes. Places to park and store equipment—

All of it needed to be planned for in advance.

"I'm glad," I murmured, finger working furiously on the button.

"What's that clicking?" Pierce said into the silence.

I froze. "I'm in Iceland."

A beat then, "And that involves clicking, how?"

"I'm scouting," I said. "Or rather, I'm scouting my scouted locations so that I can make sure they're up to snuff."

Pierce chuckled. "You know, most executive producers of your stature sit at home and just lend their names to projects. They don't take fourteen-hour plane rides halfway around the globe to scout locations."

"I'm not most producers," I said, striding back over to the car and telling my driver to proceed to the next location. "It's my money," I told Pierce, "which means that if I want to keep it, then I'd better know where it's going."

"No," he said as I buckled in, "it's because you love it."

A tingle shot down to my stomach.

In the five years since we'd slept together, I'd gotten to know Pierce quite well. You couldn't move in the same circles for extended periods of time and *not* get to know someone. Well, *I* couldn't, especially when that someone was a person I liked.

"Don't try to deny it," he said lightly. "You're an excellent producer because you love what you do . . . and also because you're crazy enough to fly halfway around the world on no sleep just to scout out locations that have already been scouted."

"I slept on the plane."

Pierce chuckled. "You're also excellent at avoiding any kind of conversation that might bring up anything personal about you."

Smart man.

Part of why I liked him so much. In fact, my appreciation for all things Pierce Daniels was almost enough to warrant breaking my rule of keeping all personal relationships temporary. Light. Easy. No drama.

Except, one night hadn't been nearly enough for my body . . . or my mind.

Not that it changed anything.

I was forty-two years old. I lived and breathed my work. There wasn't room for anything else.

"I'm glad you liked it," I said.

There was a sigh. "Really good at deflecting," he murmured then louder, "Yes, I liked it. I'm also hoping the fact that you sent it with a terrified intern to my front door at midnight means that you both want me to sign on and also that the rights have been optioned already."

His tone was so serious I couldn't tell if that would be a good or bad thing. So, I told him the truth. "Yes. To both." A beat before I made an offer I'd never *ever* done before, not on a project I really wanted. "But . . . I'll also step back from it if you want me to."

Silence.

Then, "Why in the hell would I want you to step back when you're the best damned producer I've ever met?" he asked, almost angry. "Is it because you don't like my work? You don't want to be associated with—"

"Pierce."

"—me because of my past films. If so—"

"*Pierce.*"

He stopped.

"I love the book, love the idea of making the film, and I love you as director for it, but also, I don't want to step on your toes. You're looking for something," I reminded him. "And I'm not sure that something is with me pulling my normal control freak production skills with you. Maybe you want—"

"I want this. I want you."

Oh.

Well, that was . . .

Not interesting exactly. Hell, who was I kidding? It was *exceptionally* interesting. At least until he went on because then, and another thing I would never admit this side of alive, but I was mildly disappointed.

"I want the most talented producer in film working on this project, and I want her to allow me to direct it," he said. "This isn't about me having some sort of ego trip and having to bring a project to fruition by myself. I *like* working with a team. I *like* the process."

I pushed the disappointment away. This was why I worked and lived in temporaries.

Anything deeper got in the way.

"Good," I said. "It's settled then. I'll reach out to my assistant, have her schedule some time so we can get the ball rolling."

He blew out a breath, one that I would have said sounded frustrated if not for his enthusiastic tone that followed it. "Sounds good, Artie," he said. "Thanks for thinking of me. I can't wait to get started."

"Me neither," I murmured, saying goodbye and hanging up.

I couldn't wait.

Not a lie.

But also dangerously close to *not* temporary.

Shit.

SIX

Pierce, Nine Months Later

HER HAIR WAS A MESS, an absolute mass of blond locks tangling across her face as the wind whipped up the cliffs.

All I could see were snippets of Artie's features—the corner of a plump, red mouth, one arching blond brow, a glimpse of an arctic blue eye.

And she was still the most beautiful thing I'd ever had the luxury of witnessing.

"I'm really loving the fact that my hair tie snapped," she muttered, wrestling with her hair. Frankly, I was surprised she didn't have an army of them at her disposal, since she was normally so prepared and put together. However, there was something off about Artie today, something I'd noticed when we'd set out scouting that morning. It wasn't fragile, exactly, but almost . . . precarious, as though she needed cheering up.

I'd done a decent job of that thus far, the shadows receding from her eyes, a smile creeping into the edges of her lips. She'd definitely been laughing at my crappy jokes during the last ten minutes of the drive.

"Here," I murmured, unable to watch her struggle with her hair any longer. I gathered the locks at her nape and twisted them into a quick braid that I tied off with a rubber band I had around my wrist. My sisters would probably kill me for daring to put the strip of tangle-inducing, albeit effective at containment, material into another woman's hair.

But desperate times called for desperate measures.

I could pray for forgiveness to the hair gods later.

"Where'd you learn how to do that?" she asked, curiosity dancing across her face.

That was much better than sad, and so I shared. "My sisters."

"I didn't know you had sisters."

I grinned, kept sharing. "I'm the baby of the family," I told her. "They're much older—as I love to remind them—and settled with kids of their own."

"That's nice." She smiled. "Are they in L.A.?"

"God no." I mock-shuddered. "They want nothing to do with the Hollywood crowd. Not that they're not proud of me. It's just..."

"A lot."

"Yeah. That." I shrugged. "And they've got kids of their own. Obligations and partners and their own jobs. I'm just the little brother they tortured by making me play dress-up."

She held up the braid I'd put into her hair. "Well, I definitely benefited from all that dress-up experience, so if I ever meet them, I'll have to thank them."

"They'd love that," I said with a smirk. "They like your movies more than mine."

"Seems to be a lot of that going around."

I mock-glared. "Sisters are the worst."

"I happen to think they have impeccable taste." She smiled beatifically. "But seriously, how was it growing up as the baby?"

"It had its perks. Besides imparting the braiding skills, they looked out for me and didn't make me feel *too* awful when I tried to trail along after them and their friends."

"How much older are they?"

"Ten and twelve years."

"Oh fuck."

My feet skittered to a stop, eyes darting around. "What? What's the matter?"

"Nothing."

"Artie."

"It's nothing."

I tugged at her braid. "Nice try with the lies, but don't try and bullshit a bullshitter."

We stared off for several minutes before she caved. "Fine." She rolled her eyes. "But the only reason I'm telling you this at all is because we've always been honest with each other."

"Brutally so," I grumbled.

She rested her head on my shoulder, fluttered her eyelashes up at me. "You love my honesty."

"Is that what I've been feeling?" I narrowed my eyes. "Loving your honesty when you nixed my rewrite of Bethany's death scene?"

"You'll love it when the reviews come in raving about it."

"That's if Eden can do it."

"Eden will nail it." Artie nodded ahead. "Come on and take a look at this outcropping. When I saw the pictures, I thought it would be perfect for the opening."

I followed her, spent all of three seconds looking and knew immediately she was right. We'd pan up the cliffs, watch the wind whipping around the heroine's hair, her clothes, witness the paper flying from her hand and spinning and tumbling over the edge. "You're right."

She grinned, clasped her hands to her chest. "I do love it when you're honest with me."

Honest, as in I often still woke up hard after dreaming about her all night? Or maybe honest as in I still jerked off to the little sounds she'd made when I'd licked her pussy?

Instead of asking her either of those questions, I brought us back to the previous topic, the one she'd so masterfully avoided. "So, what were you *oh fucking* about before?"

She sighed. "I hate it when you're smart."

"Lie."

Another sigh. "I also hate that you have two older sisters that are younger than me."

"Age is just a number."

"Quoting my mantra back to me doesn't discount the fact that I slept with their baby brother and they're *younger* than me."

My pulse picked up. We didn't talk about our night together, didn't even allude to it. Not ever. That she'd mentioned it—

"Who cares that they're younger?" I asked carefully.

Artie shrugged. "I don't, not really. Just that it's the truth, and I'm a woman over forty, which means that half of society already hates me and the other half thinks that I'm a shriveled up prune."

My brows drew together. "I'm part of society, and I don't think that."

"Okay, so *one* percent of society thinks I'm all right."

"Artie." I touched her arm. "You're beautiful and capable and smart—"

She groaned, batted me away. "Don't try to be logical when I'm having a weak moment."

"You're far from weak."

She sighed. "And you're too damned sweet and honest, but

I'll take the compliment anyway." She visibly shook off her insecurity, replacing it with a mask I knew too well—calm and charming and totally superficial. "I'm just having a weird day. Must be all these hormones, you know how they flare in old age," she added with a chuckle.

I hated it, hated the mask, hated the way she used it to prevent her from having to present herself to the world.

But it also wasn't my place to push.

She'd chosen to put the distance between us, and that was where it would stay. I didn't have any right to barge through barriers, not when our intimacy hadn't extended to more than one night. Plus, now that we were working together, it was even more critical that the distance stay in place. We needed to be collaborators, friends, soundboards, but we also shouldn't be anything more than that.

Not the right time.

Even if I wished it was.

"Just be happy you weren't living here two hundred years ago," I said, purposefully going along with the reappearance of Artie's mask and allowing her to change the subject. Vibrant blue eyes met mine, and she proved that whatever chemistry we had that made us seem to always be on the same wavelength was still in effect.

"Because of the dresses."

"Yup," I said, reaching out for her braid and pretending to make it flap in the breeze. "The fabric would blow you and all this hair right off the cliffs."

She grinned. "Just in time for a dashing hero to dive to my rescue."

I snorted. "More like, she'd save herself."

Artie laughed and leaned close enough that I could smell the soft, floral scent of her shampoo. "You're learning." She nudged me with her shoulder. "But alas, those dresses were heavy, especially when they got wet. I think she'd need that dashing hero to swoop in and save the day."

"Should we test that theory?" I teased, giving her a mock-shove toward the edge. "I bet those jeans will absorb a lot of water."

"Don't you dare!" she said on a gasp, darting away from me.

"Come on," I cajoled. "It's not *that* far of a jump."

"Not that far?" She swept out her arm. "It's like fifty feet!"

"Meh." I snagged her arm, lightly tugging her back to the cliffs. By now, we were a good ten feet from the edge, but she shrieked and yanked away from me.

"So not funny, Pierce."

"From my angle, it was hilarious." She rolled her eyes, spinning on a huff. "Careful," I warned, seeing she was headed for some loose rocks.

"Nice try—"

She slipped.

What happened next was something my mind could barely process, let alone my body ever having hope of replicating it. I lurched forward, grabbing Artie by the waist, attempting to steady her so she didn't take a header in the sharp rocks, but she was off-balance, limbs flailing . . . which meant that her fist flew up and clocked me right in the eye. I groaned, lost my grip on her, and our feet got tangled, propelling us to a painful collision with the rocky ground.

The only reason I was able to hold on to my man card in the clusterfuck of limbs was because I managed to grab her arm and spin us slightly, so I took the brunt of the impact, Artie landing hard on my stomach.

We lay there for a few moments, me with a smarting eye, an aching set of butt cheeks, and her . . . thinking who knew what? Eventually, though, I managed to squeeze out. "Are you okay?"

She groaned. "My ass."

I could second that notion. "Want me to pick us up a pair of those donut pillows?"

"Hilarious," she muttered. "This is your fault." She started to push out of the circle of my arms then stopped, staring out at the cliffs. "Can you imagine how pissed our insurance company would have been if we fell off the fucking cliff?"

I bit back a laugh, heart settling now that I'd managed to get us out of the situation relatively unscathed—asses and left eye aside. "Probably really pissed," I agreed, sitting up and taking her with me. "But I don't know why you're blaming me. I'm not the one who decided to tap dance through some loose rocks."

"Oh, maybe because someone was threatening to throw me off a cliff in order to test his hero skills."

I snorted as Artie slowly stood, stretching out her spine with a wince. "As if you thought I was serious."

"Fair point," she muttered. "Maybe I *do* need a hero to come in and save the day, since I can't even walk on a flat surf—oh my God! *Pierce.* Your eye."

I brought my hand up, gently palpated the skin around it. "It's fine."

"It's already purple! Oh shit, I *hurt* you." Her hands began flapping over my chest and face. "Oh my God. It's already bruising, and I—"

"It's *fine.*" I captured her hands. "Bonus is I'm going to have a hell of a story to lord over you the next few years."

She froze and for the first time in the five-plus years I'd known her, Artie's eyes filled with tears that weren't because of a film or a book or a script. "I'm sorry," she said. "I hurt you and —" She sniffed as one glistening tear escaped. "I—*fuck.*" Jerking her hands back, she put them over her face. "I can't believe I-I did that."

"Hey. *Hey,*" I repeated, tugging at her hands when she wouldn't look at me. "*Artie.*"

She shoved me back and strode away.

I stared after her for a few seconds, trying to figure out why she was so upset. It was clearly an accident, and one I'd thought we'd laugh about for years to come. But she wasn't laughing. In fact, she was so close to distraught that my stomach was twisting itself into knots. There was something else going on here. I moved, pushing up to my feet, and crossing over to her.

"Artemis," I said softly.

Her chin dropped to her chest for several seconds. Then she almost seemed to force herself to look at me.

The bottom fell out of my heart at the tear tracks on her cheeks, the reddened eyes, the remorse in her expression. "I didn't mean to hit you," she said. "I swear I didn't. It was an a-accident."

I dropped my hands to her shoulders, lightly squeezing. "I *know* that," I murmured. "It's just . . . *you* don't seem to."

Her lids closed. "I hurt you."

"Babe. It was an accident."

"That doesn't make it right," she snapped.

"And beating yourself up until your insides are black and blue for something you didn't mean to do *is*?"

She shook her head. "You don't understand."

"Then *tell* me, sweetheart," I said. "Explain to me why you accidentally hitting me as you tripped and fell is something that's horrible and—"

"Because my dad did it, okay?" She pulled out of my hold and paced away, this time without the flailing and subsequent black eye. "He'd say it was an accident. He'd pretend that my mom or I fell or that something stupid and innocuous happened and we were just . . . too fucking *klutzy* to not get hurt and"—her voice dropped—"it would always be an *accident*."

Her chest was rising and falling like she'd run a marathon.

And I was standing there, shocked by the revelation and unable to say a fucking thing.

"I ran into doorknobs, slipped and fell in the tub, tripped at the park." She shook her head, voice dropping so it was almost inaudible. "So many *fucking* accidents."

Finally, I got my shit together. "It's not your fault."

She scoffed. "It was *my* hand that hit you."

"Not that, Artie," I said gently. "What your dad did is not your fault."

Her face crumpled and for a horrible few seconds, I thought that I'd said the wrong thing. But then she closed the distance between us and buried her face in my throat. Instinctively, my arms wrapped around her, holding her close.

I thought she'd cry, that tears would soak through my shirt, cooling the skin of my chest. Instead, I held her as her breaths rattled through her chest, as hot puffs of air beat against my neck, as she shuddered and vibrated and then finally, *finally* relaxed in my arms.

"I'm sorry," she whispered, forehead to my collarbone, tone beyond fragile.

"You have absolutely nothing to be sorry about."

Her shoulders rose and fell as she took one more deep inhale then let it out. "Normally, I'm not like this."

"Artie." I pulled back, crouched a little to meet her gaze. "You don't owe me an explanation just because I'm here and saw . . ."

Whatever the fuck I'd just witnessed.

"Today is the day I lost her." She turned away, spine stiff, braid I'd put in her hair less than fifteen minutes before disheveled and flopping over her shoulder.

I hesitated, took Artie's hand. "Lost who, sweetheart?"

"My mom."

SEVEN

Artie

WHAT THE FUCK was I doing?

"We should go," I declared, starting to run a hand through my hair and stopping when I remembered it was braided.

That Pierce had braided it.

What the fuck was *that?*

He'd braided my—

Not the point. What was critically important at this juncture was that I pulled my shit together and we got back to making a fucking movie.

"I had a word with Frank about budget," I said, hightailing it to the car, not even checking that Pierce was following me. Thankfully, though, I heard his footsteps crunching along behind me when I paused for breath. "He thinks we'd be better off going with Rhonda for cinematography, even though that would put us a bit over. She's one of the best, and a spot just opened up in her schedule."

Silence.

Don't look behind me, don't look behind—

I looked behind me.

Pierce had stopped about five feet back, crossing his arms over his chest. I opened my mouth, readying a deflection, attempting to draw us down into movie talk and not toward my blurt on the cliffside.

I should have known better than to think I'd be able to work him.

Too smart, too quick, too fucking perfect.

So much so that he'd stuck in my head over the last five years, not staying shut in the locked box of my brain. I'd be in Australia and think, he'd love to see the waves breaking on the shore, know that he'd compare them to his time spent shooting in Hawaii. Then I'd be in Italy and imagine him hanging off a crane to capture just the right angle of a crumbling building. Or at an award's show and think that he'd fit in way better if he could just understand that he was the most talented guy in the room.

But then I'd tuck it all down, lock it all safely away . . . and I'd move on.

It's what I did.

Pierce knew that.

He just wasn't going to let it slide today. "Rhonda would be amazing," he said before I could make some comment dragging us further from my meltdown. "But that's not what we should be talking about, is it?"

"It's the only pertinent conversation we'll be having for the time being."

"You mean discussing the movie as a way to avoid whatever the fuck all that just was."

"Yes."

His mouth was parted, an argument to press further, no doubt already on the tip of his tongue. At my answer, his teeth clicked closed.

I sighed. "Should I reiterate that you just stated I don't owe you an explanation?"

He closed the distance between us. "That's right," he said, surprising me.

I'd expected an argument about how things change and how I need to lay all my troubles with the big, bad man so I don't have to worry my pretty little head.

"Your past is your past. *It's yours.*" He sighed. "However, maybe the fucking courteous thing to do would be to explain why your past is playing so hard into today. We're friends, Artie. That means I'm here for you."

So easy.

It would be *so easy* to just tell him everything, to confide in him about my past, my dead mother, my incarcerated father, the years I'd spent in Canada with them, hiding from our troubles.

But I didn't talk about it.

And most especially, I couldn't talk about it today. Not when *this* day made the loss of my mom all that fresher.

So, I lifted my chin and reached for the passenger's side door. "If we're really friends," I said, pulling it open and plunking myself into the seat, "then we'll get back to what's really important, what's the *only* important thing, and that's filming this movie."

Pierce bent, studying me through the window on the driver's side for several awkward seconds before his face went blank and he opened his own door, plunking into his own seat. "The movie," he murmured, buckling in. "You want to just focus on making the film. Got it." A nod. "I can shut up and just fucking work."

Guilt warred with self-preservation. "Pierce—"

He stuck the key in the ignition, turned on the car, and drove us to the next location.

In silence.

I tried to convince myself it was better this way.

IT WAS AFTER MIDNIGHT, the grasping talons of the past finally relenting, the painful memories finally releasing their hold on my heart and mind.

Twenty years since I'd lost her.

Twenty fucking years.

Sighing, I slipped on a sweatshirt, shoved my feet into my UGGs, and wrestled my hair into a lopsided bun that was a hell of a lot messier than the braid Pierce had woven earlier that day.

Or yesterday, I supposed.

Either way, I was *this* close—cue mental fingers held just a pinch apart—to a hot mess, but felt so raw inside that I didn't give a damn how I looked. I needed a drink. I needed to forget for another three hundred and sixty-five days.

I needed to compartmentalize away what I'd told Pierce.

How I'd acted.

How critically embarrassed I was.

Sighing, I slipped out of the hotel room and padded down the hall to the stairs. The bar should still be open. I'd get a drink or two, liquor my brain up enough that I could sleep, and then everything would look better after eight horizontal hours.

Two flights of stairs down led me to the lobby, and I walked through, glad that it was deserted and that the bar was nearly so, only a couple of patrons at a table on the far side. I chose the corner furthest from them and sat, ordering a whiskey sour.

Because that was my mom's drink.

And because it seemed like an appropriate end to the day.

Thankfully, the bartender seemed to recognize I wasn't fit for human consumption and poured the drink quickly, setting it on the bar top, and retreating to the other end, giving me my space.

There was a big tip coming her way.

Sighing, I took a big swig, letting the alcohol burn a trail down my esophagus, warming me slowly from the inside out, and waiting for the pleasant buzz to trail across my mind, dulling the final throb of my childhood.

I always thought I was so together and recovered from the trauma of my upbringing. Then this day would come, and I would feel flayed to the core all over again. Lifting the glass, I took another sip, the burn less this time, the lovely numbing fog more encompassing.

This day.

I usually didn't work on this day.

Or if I did, I worked alone.

I slurped down the final drops, barely signaled to the bartender before she'd dropped the refill in front of me and disappeared again.

Definitely a big tip. Huge, even.

I crossed my arms on the bar top, resting my cheek against one as I ran a finger from the other around and around the smoothed ring at the top of the glass.

So, why hadn't I forced the issue today? Why hadn't I insisted on being alone?

Pierce.

I figured he'd be a good distraction and with our film moving forward in rapid succession, shooting just on the horizon, we'd needed to take advantage of having a few days of clear schedules to lock in the final details.

No. Not it.

Or not *all* of it.

I'd wanted to see him. I liked him. He was funny and charming and . . . I'd given in to my inner idiotic desires for him.

I'd had a weak moment in allowing it to happen and an even weaker moment when disclosing all I'd disclosed.

Fuck.

There was a reason I'd taken a hiatus from the industry for several years. To distance myself from the news reports, from the media trailing me during the trial. Yes, the truth was out there, never completely hidden, and I'd had to address it a lot, especially when I'd first become successful. Hell, it was right there under the 'Personal Life' section on my *Wikipedia* page. But I'd also found that when something was common knowledge for a while in Hollywood, it tended to become less sensationalized and more old news.

There was always a newer train wreck to observe.

Mine was old. And over forty.

Snorting, I lifted enough to take a sip from the glass before dropping my head back down to my arms.

Already my limbs felt loose, relaxed. I'd finish the drink, find my bed, and seal away the rest of the memories.

Good plan.

And go.

Unfortunately, just as I'd raised the glass to my lips again, someone sat on the barstool next to me.

EIGHT

Pierce

HAIR BOUND up tight and reckless, shoulders slumped, eyes closed, exhaustion playing over her features.

Still gorgeous.

Still pathetically hung up on her.

The first being Artie. The second me.

"Want another?" I asked when she opened her eyes to stare up at me.

Silence for so long that I almost would have thought she'd fallen asleep, if not for the way those deep blue eyes continued to stare at me. They were dulled, and I wasn't sure if it was from the alcohol or if it was from pain.

Then she blinked.

And just like that, they brightened. "Sure," she said, pushing up. "A cute guy wants to buy me a drink, I'm all for it." She lifted a hand, gestured to the bartender.

"Don't do that," I murmured, setting my palm on her forearm.

I saw through it now, and maybe I'd never have what I truly

wanted with her, maybe I would always be relegated to friend and coworker, but I physically could not stand the idea of her hiding her true self from me.

"Do what?" She forced a laugh. "Make you actually follow through with buying me a drink? *Of course*, I'm going to do that, you silly man."

A drink slid in front of Artie, and I handed the bartender a few bills along with a murmured, "Thanks."

"You want anything?" the bartender asked me, a towel thrown over one shoulder.

"I'm good."

With a nod, she retreated back to the other end of the bar.

I turned back to Artie.

She deliberately kept her eyes on her glass, but at least the cheery, fake façade had faded. I weighed the moment, trying to decide if I should wade into the fray or if I should just keep my fucking mouth shut.

In the end, I couldn't not say anything.

"I know what yesterday was to you."

She inhaled so quickly that her breath whistled between her teeth. "Pierce—"

"You don't have to say anything," I hurried to say, wanting her to understand I wasn't trying to force her to discuss something painful or uncomfortable. "Just . . . I know why it was hard. And"—I ran the back of my hand over her cheek—"I understand, or well, understand as much as I can, not having been through it." I sucked in a breath. "My point is, you don't have to fake it with me, okay? Be sad. Drink. Curse. Shove me off a fucking cliff if you want. Just don't feel like you have to be anything but *you* when you're with me."

Tears pooled within those blue depths before she shifted, eyes focused behind the bar, rather than on me.

She stayed in that position for a long, long time.

Then her shoulders dropped, her arms refolded, and her head stacked back down on top of them. Her sigh was long and drawn out and slow, her words, when they finally came, so quiet I had to strain to hear them.

"Thank you."

I rested my hand on her elbow, replied just as softly, "You're welcome."

We sat there for a long time, not talking, not even looking at each other, just two people in the universe propped next to each another, one giving comfort, one accepting it.

Until finally, Artie's glass was empty.

"Another?"

She shook her head. "Sleep."

Weaving my arm around her waist, I guided her from the stool then over to the elevators and up to her room.

"Sleep well, sweetheart," I murmured.

A nod, manicured nails flashing as she pushed through the door then paused. "Pierce?"

I'd stepped back, hands thrust into my pockets. "Yeah?"

"Thanks."

"None needed."

Eyes to the ground then up to mine. "They're needed," she murmured. "I—" A short, sharp breath. "I—"

When she faltered again, I gently pried her fingers off the door.

"No explanations. No thanks." I nudged her inside. "Just . . . friends."

She swallowed, blinked rapidly. "Just friends."

Grabbing the knob, I murmured, "Good night," and closed the door just as she replied in turn.

I listened to her flip the dead bolt, to the sound of her feet moving away.

I listened to her movements for a long time because it was

better than focusing on how miserable we both had sounded about the "just friends." Me, I understood I was pining. Artie? She was just vulnerable and upset because of her past. If I allowed myself to think even for one second that things might possibly be different for us, I'd do something really fucking crazy.

I couldn't do crazy.

Not to her. Not for me. Not for this project.

Those were the thoughts that finally got my feet moving down the hall and to my own room. They were the reason I was able to shove away the urge to go back and knock on Artie's door, to pull her into my arms and just hold her until her pain faded.

They were the reason I didn't return to shoulder however much of her pain she'd let me carry.

Because it wasn't right, wasn't what she wanted, wasn't what I could ever have.

I just needed to get that through my thick skull.

And maybe, also through my heart.

I NEEDN'T HAVE WORRIED about getting the previous night's sentiments through my mind if I'd known what I'd wake to.

That being, Artie gone.

Me alone in a hotel in the middle of Scotland.

I understood.

We'd breached some sort of inner barrier in her at the bar that night, at the cliffs the day before. She was vulnerable and running, even though she'd left a note with the front desk saying that she'd been called into an emergency meeting back in the States and would catch back up with me soon.

She'd come back.

I knew that she was too much of a professional to leave me flapping in the wind, but I also knew enough about her after almost six years to recognize she'd come back with several new layers of protective armor.

Sighing, but knowing that any other reality was impossible, I buckled down and methodically went through the remainder of my required tasks in Scotland. I finished approving the locations, spoke to the local producer who'd be in charge of filming there, signed off on the use of Rhonda as Director of Cinematography.

I did what I did best.

Forgot the messy and focused on the project at hand.

Filming was beginning in less than a month, and I wouldn't allow whatever had happened between Artie and me to jeopardize that.

This was too important to both of us. I could hold down the fort.

But I couldn't lie and say I didn't miss having her there holding it down with me.

L.A., in the wintertime, was a mindfuck.

Or maybe that was because I'd finished my week in Scotland and had returned to sunny California, to eighty-degree weather and sunshine instead of biting wind and chilling rain, and my body hadn't adjusted to the fact that I needed shorts instead of parkas.

It was a few days before Thanksgiving and my family was in town, readying to celebrate an early Christmas on the West Coast with me because I would be filming *Carrot* over the holiday.

Best title ever.

Especially since the lead, Eden, had bright red hair.

A girl from a tiny village in Scotland somehow finding herself at the center of the Allies efforts during WWII, stumbling through life as she figured shit out. It was coming of age. It was historical. It was painful to read. It was . . . really fucking real.

Almost *too* real, but that would be *my* job to balance the knife's edge of reality and fantasy and history in order to take the viewer along for a ride.

If that wasn't a comparison for my life, then I had no clue what was.

Reality vs. fantasy vs past.

Artie had called me that night after she'd left, all cheerful and sweet, apologizing for having to skip out and thanking me profusely for helming the visits and coordinating with the local producer.

But all I could see was fear.

Distance.

Avoidance.

Except, she didn't *seem* to be avoiding me. She'd continued checking in daily, had sent me texts with pictures and thoughts.

So, maybe I was the one who'd fallen to the wrong side of reality.

Maybe I needed to stop living in this fantasy that one day Artie would look at me and realize that instead of pushing me away, she wanted to hold me close.

Because, fuck, it had been almost six years since we'd first sat down for lunch together. And I was still here, awed by her, but also spinning in circles because I'd tasted her once and hadn't gotten my fill.

I'd never get my fill.

Which meant I needed to shove that shit down and move on.

Sighing, I parked my car and walked over to baggage claim, making sure to pick up two luggage carts. My family—all of them, both sisters, mom and dad, spouses, and various nieces and nephews—would come with a lot of bags. Glancing at the screen, I checked and saw that their flight had already landed, so I hurried over to where they'd come out.

I saw my nephew Grayson first, blond curls flopping as he jumped next to my sister Marie, holding one hand as he did so. Her arm jerked, but she almost seemed not to notice, so swept up in the kindergartner's excitement.

Well, that and she was holding my newest nephew, one-year-old Chase, in her arms, so Grayson didn't exactly have her full attention.

They were trailed by Marie's husband, Joe, who was holding the hands of their four-year-old twins, Elliot and Ella—side note: their names were an ode to how truly evil Marie was for making their names a perpetual tongue twister.

See? Kids. Loads of them. And that wasn't even counting my other sister, Kate, who was married to Hank and had a two-year-old daughter, Gabriella, and a five-year-old son, Thomas.

They, along with my mom and dad, paraded down the path leading past the TSA agent and burst through to the waiting area in a flurry of noise, strollers, and children.

Grayson was the first to spot me, shouting, "Uncle Pierce!" and tearing away from Marie to come barreling toward me.

"Gray!" I said, bracing myself for impact before sweeping him up and into my arms. "Hey, bud. How are you?"

"I got pretzels!"

Assuming that was six-year-old speak for awesome, I hugged him tight for the moment he allowed me then released the squirming mass of muscle back to the ground. Thomas was right there, but because he tended toward shy—and with a cousin like Grayson to steal the spotlight that wasn't really a surprise—I didn't immediately reach forward to hug him. Instead, I crouched down and held up a palm for a high-five.

Thomas gave me one before throwing his arms around my neck and demanding, "Up."

That I could do.

Thirty seconds with a six-year-old and a five-year-old and I was already feeling more balanced.

"Did you get pretzels, too?"

"Yup. Two bags."

"They were generous," Marie said, stepping close enough to press a kiss to my cheek. "Probably because it was the only way to get this brood to shut up." She leaned back, almost taking my ear with her, not realizing that little Chase had hold of it. "Whoops, sorry," she muttered, releasing it before fixing me with a glare. "You shouldn't have upgraded us."

I shrugged, quickly made the rounds of hugs and kisses with Kate and my mom and dad. Thomas kept his arms firmly locked, so I also completed my quote-unquote bro hugs—as Marie called them—with Hank and Joe with Thomas in my arms. "I would have gotten you guys into first class, but you can't seem to stop pushing out kids."

Marie snorted. Kate smacked me before patting Thomas on the head. "These guys are wonderful."

"I bet first class is, too," Marie joked, dreamily batting her eyelashes for a moment.

"Thank you," Kate said. "I agree with Marie that you *shouldn't* have upgraded us to business class, but the extra room did make it easier."

"Next time I'll charter you guys a plane," I said. "God knows you have enough people to fill it."

"You will not!" my mom said on a gasp. "That's your money, Pierce. You earned it."

Because this was an ongoing argument with my family, I

just set Thomas down so he could help me push one of the luggage carts over to baggage claim. They didn't get that they were here because of me, because my schedule made it so I wouldn't be home for Christmas. They didn't get that I was in the position I was in because *they'd* made it possible.

"Not gonna win this one, son," my dad said, a smile teasing the corners of his mouth. "Might as well let your mother have her way."

I nodded, though I didn't necessarily agree.

One of these days, I was just going to book them a trip somewhere tropical, not just transportation out to see me because my schedule messed up the family celebration. Then I was going to force them to accept my generosity and like it. I snorted. Yeah, sure, that was going to happen. Hank grabbed the second cart and we noisily made our way to the carousel. Thomas got over his shy and was running around with the twins and Grayson while my mom and Kate attempted to corral them.

My cell buzzed just after we'd retrieved the car seats from oversized baggage, and I pulled it out, checking the text and thankful I'd had the foresight to have foreseen this amount of airport chaos.

"My assistant is here with one of the vans," I told my dad. "Do you guys want to get the kids loaded and then head back to my place?"

"Van?" Hank asked. "I thought we'd just take a Lyft." Almost as quickly as the words came out of his mouth, he shook his head. "I'm an idiot. Of course, we wouldn't fit."

I released the brake on the cart. "I'll start in with car seats."

"I'll help," my dad said, picking up the hefty one that would secure Chase. "Let's go."

Having been back to visit with my family many times since they'd had kids, I was well-familiar with the installation process. Not that being familiar meant much when it came down to struggling with buckles and straps and negotiating three seats into the back of a minivan.

But ten minutes later, my assistant, Shelby, had left to retrieve the second van, and my dad and I had five seats installed, three kids strapped in, and the two more on their way. Thomas had asked to ride with me, and since he was the calmest kid of the bunch, I'd agreed.

Plus, I enjoyed the things he said.

"You're a God," Marie said, pressing a kiss to my cheek and slipping into the middle center seat to run point over the brood. My dad got behind the wheel, Kate into the passenger's seat.

"I'm not playing rock-paper-scissors with you anymore," Marie muttered, but she was already masterfully doling out snacks and books and toys.

I handed Kate my house keys, made sure they knew where they were going then started to head back inside to help Hank and Joe get the rest of the bags.

My feet skidded to a stop about two inches inside the door.

Artie.

My mom.

Talking.

And a photographer nearby, camera up as he rapidly snapped pictures.

"Pierce," my mom said with a huge wave. "Look who I found! Artemis."

"Shit," I muttered, hurrying over, seeing a few people glance up in recognition. Even when I was trying to put Artie out of my head, she still found ways to invade my life. Not fair, since I figured that my mom had been the determining factor in their conversation, but seeing her after what had happened in Scotland made me grumbly.

"Hey," Artie said as I leaned in and kissed both of her

cheeks. "It looks like you're about to be inundated for the holiday."

"We're celebrating Christmas early," my mom gushed, Thomas clutching at her leg. "Because Pierce won't be able to make it home for the holiday. But I guess you'd know that already, considering you're the reason."

Artie had been smiling, but the last had her eyes dimming. "Oh, I'm sorry. I could—"

My mom seemed to realize she'd made a mistake. She picked up Artie's hand, squeezed it lightly. "I'm sorry, dear. I didn't mean it like that. We're thrilled you two are working together." Her voice dropped to a stage whisper. "Don't tell Pierce, but *Second Chances* is my favorite film of all time."

Artie laughed, a tinkling sound that slid down my spine, relaxing me. "Thanks for the love, Mom," I said, mock-pouting, and turned to the woman who never failed to make my pulse speed up. "We tease a lot in this family."

My mom nodded. "Can't take anything we say seriously."

Artie smiled. "I'm guessing I have you to thank for why Pierce has such a good sense of humor."

"Of course, dear."

She chuckled, readjusted the grip on her carry-on's handle. "Well, I should be going," she murmured. "I'm about to head home and drown myself in reality television and wine."

I knew the expression on my mom's face spelled trouble, even before the words drifted out of her mouth.

"You should meet us for dinner later," she said, or rather, ordered.

"Um." Artie was taken aback, tired eyes flashing to mine.

"Mom, she's tired and had a long week. I bet she wants to go home and relax without a brood of Daniels making her ears bleed."

"If she's tired, then she needs a home-cooked meal and to relax."

Artie slid back. "I'm just going to order in," she said.

"Nonsense!" my mom declared. "I'm cooking my world-famous meatloaf and biscuits, and there will be enough to feed an army. You should come. I'm dying to hear about your latest project. How was Zane Potter to work with?"

Panic in Artie's expression.

"*Mom.*"

"What?"

I shot her a look that had any further protests dying on her lips. "Artie's tired."

My mom's expression fell, which made me feel like shit, but also, unfortunately, I knew it had to be done. She came on too strong, didn't realize it, and was making Artemis uncomfortable.

"Oh," my mom said, voice dropping. "Of course, she's tired. I'm sorry." A forced smile. "Some other time."

She bent and began fussing with the bags.

Aw. Fuck.

Stifling a sigh, because there was nothing to be done for it right then, I turned to Artie, "I'll talk to you late—"

"Actually, meatloaf sounds amazing."

I blinked, jaw falling open.

My mom's head jerked up. "Really?"

Artie nodded. "What time are you eating?"

"With this horrible L.A. traffic, maybe six?"

"I feel you on the traffic," Artie said with a smile. "Six sounds great. What can I bring?"

"Artie—" I began.

Neither of them acknowledged me.

"Nothing, dear. Just yourself."

"Nonsense. I can't show up empty-handed."

"Mom—"

Still ignoring me.

"Fine," my mom said with a happy smile. She loved nothing more than a polite guest, and showing up with a hostess gift was a surefire way to start on the correct foot with her. "How about a bottle of that wine you were speaking of earlier?"

Artie grinned. "I can do that. Red or white?"

"Yes."

Artie burst out laughing. "Okay, so both." Her phone beeped in her hand, and she glanced down at the screen before announcing, "My car's here. I'll see you two later."

She waved and headed toward the doors.

"Be right back," I said to my mom, hurrying after Artie. "Hey"—I caught her arm just outside the doors—"you don't have to—"

A smile that didn't completely reach her eyes. "I wasn't joking, Pierce, meatloaf sounds awesome."

"You're lying."

She sighed. "No one can make me do something I don't want to."

"But—"

"I know we had a . . . an odd moment in Scotland. But I'm fine now. And I mean it. If I didn't want to come meet your family, I would be heading home, pajamas bound right at this moment."

"There will be kids there."

"I saw him. He's adorable."

"Five more. None older than six."

Her eyes widened, but she nodded. "Okay, great. I love kids."

"You say that now."

She patted my cheek, smiling again though this time it was finally real, that warmth seeping into her blue eyes. "I can't wait to get all of the embarrassing stories from your sisters. Starting with how exactly they taught you to braid."

I groaned.

"It'll be great," she said. "You'll see."

Why did I feel like those were famous last words?

NINE

Artie

OKAY, so I had a minor freak out on the 405.

But it was gone by the time I drove through the meandering roads of Brentwood. Pierce's house was smaller than some of the neighbors', but I thought its location couldn't be beat. Positioned at the end of a cul-de-sac, he only had neighbors on one side, and because of the way the lots matched up, even that house was set far away.

Space was often at a premium in L.A., but Pierce had made a smart call with this purchase.

Plus, the view was insane.

Rolling hills, green oak trees dotting their tops, the city in the distance. He'd even avoided a good portion of the smog.

Smart man.

And that was right about the point I remembered I was meeting his family.

Seriously. What the absolute fuck was I doing?

First, I'd had a meltdown in Scotland, freaking out about something that was clearly an accident, then telling him things I never should have confided, *then* I'd gotten drunk, after which I'd done the equivalent of a walk of shame, except it was a calling-in-a-private-plane-so-I-could-get-the-fuck-out of shame, leaving him with work *I* should have been doing.

It was a clusterfuck.

And now I was going to his house to meet his family.

Of all the idiotic things I'd done in my life, I seemed to just be continuing to add to the pile this week.

Brilliant.

But his mom's face had dropped after Pierce had stepped in. Though I gave the man credit, he'd seen I was uncomfortable, had taken measures to stop it from happening. That took a backbone and even more so when the person that required the halting was a parent, most especially a mother.

Still, her expression had morphed. She was lovely and energetic and sweet . . . and disappointed because of me.

I was a lot of things, but I couldn't stand hurting someone like that.

No matter that this was probably going to be a disaster.

No matter that this was about as far from keeping my professional distance as possible.

No matter that part of me *wanted* to say yes the moment the offer had been made. I'd seen the way Pierce's cute little nephew had stared up at him, beyond taken with his uncle—a similar feeling I'd experienced, having gotten to know him fairly well over the last few years (I deliberately ignored the biblical type of *knowing*) and wanted to learn more about his family. I'd witnessed how excited his mom was to be in L.A. celebrating Christmas early, not because she wouldn't miss her son on the actual day, but because she was thrilled that he was living his dream.

I knew this because *my* mom had been like that.

Thrilled and proud and gentle and sweet. And pushy and wonderful and—

I couldn't disappoint Pierce's.

Read into that what I wanted.

"Stupidity, that's what," I muttered, turning into his driveway and winding my way up to his house. Two large minivans were parked in front of the garage, and I blocked one in, hoping that wouldn't create any issues later, then I reached for the bag I'd filled with six bottles of wine—three red, two white, one sparkling—and maneuvered my way out of the driver's seat.

I heard them before I saw them.

Screaming—which I assumed was of the child-based variety because of the high-pitched tone. It was interspersed with laughter, punctuated by deeper adult voices. None of the noise sounded worried and so I didn't immediately grab my cell and dial 9-1-1, which I might have done had I come across the commotion on a street corner.

Instead, I slung the bag over my shoulder, bent to pick up my purse with my other hand, and sucked in a breath.

Shoring myself for the chaos inside.

Hell, who was I kidding?

I was shoring myself against Pierce.

I might have only allowed myself one night with him, but that had been enough to devastate my defenses.

He'd wiggled his way in like a fox tail, sly and persistent, burrowing his way under my skin until I couldn't stop myself from rushing over to see him at events, from thinking about projects he might like, from . . . coming to dinner tonight.

Because I'd be kidding myself if I thought it was only about disappointing his mom.

It was about disappointing *Pierce's* mom.

And yet, I was here.

"Idiot," I muttered.

"Idiot's a bad word."

I jumped, whipping around, the bag swinging forward and almost flying off my arm, trying to locate the voice that had said that.

They were below my line of sight, so it took me a few heartbeats to see the cute little blond boy who'd been clutching Pierce's leg at the airport.

"Hi, tiny person," I said, crouching down and meeting curious blue eyes. "I'm Artie."

He wrinkled his nose. "Artie's a boy's name."

I grinned, having heard the sentiment many times over my life. "There isn't really such a thing as a boy's name or a girl's name. They're all just names."

He stopped, head tilting as he considered that.

After a few seconds, he nodded. "That makes sense."

"What's your name?"

"Thomas."

"Nice to meet you, Thomas," I said, standing and reaching up to fix the heavy bag. Maybe six bottles of wine was too much, but I hadn't wanted to bring too few, especially when Pierce had mentioned the Daniels hoard at the airport.

Hoard equated to six bottles in my mind.

"You, too," he said.

"So, want to show me—"

He ran off.

My words trailed away as he disappeared around the corner of the house. "I guess it's this way," I said, starting to follow him.

"You'd guess right."

Heat shooting down my middle, arrowing between my thighs.

Which meant that even if I hadn't recognized his voice, I would have known Pierce was standing very close. Fingers slipped under the strap of the bag, relieving me of the heavy burden. "Hey," he murmured. "You sure you're ready for this?"

"Is your mom's meatloaf really world-famous?"

"Maybe *family* famous?" Pierce said, lips twitching. "It's not as good as your pasta, but it *is* delicious."

"Then yes," I said. "I am *so* ready for this."

"It's your death wish," he said with a shrug.

"And your confidence in me is overwhelming."

"Not you," he said, tugging at my ponytail, "it's my family that's the trouble."

"Trouble, as in they're a family of ax murderers?" I teased. "I can just picture this brood of little ones with child-sized axes."

His hand dropped from my ponytail down to my shoulder. "Sometimes I really worry about you."

I laughed. "I worry about me on a daily basis."

"I worry about *Pierce*"—we turned to see a pretty blonde emerging from behind the house, holding Thomas's hand—"on a daily basis." She grinned. "You seem quite normal at first glance."

"I'm hoping that's a compliment?" I asked. I hadn't been sure what to wear, so I'd gone for something that fit in with what Pierce and his mom had been wearing at the airport—jeans, sneakers, a simple cowl-necked sweater. So far, that seemed like a good call, considering Pierce was in a T-shirt and his sister was in a similar outfit as mine, though she'd swapped the jeans for leggings.

"Definitely a compliment," she said.

I walked forward, stuck out my hand. "Hi, I'm Artie."

"It's not a boy's name," Thomas interjected, rather helpfully, I thought.

Bending, I stuck out a fist. He bumped it with his. "Thanks, bud."

"Hi, Artie, not a boy's name. I'm Kate."

We shook hands. "Nice to meet you," I said. "And thanks for letting me crash your family dinner."

"From what I heard, it's more like you were waylaid into it."

I shrugged. "So perhaps, that's more the truth of it."

Kate grinned. "Thus is the powers of moms. Well, let me just invite you to come on into a house that isn't mine." She swept a hand down the path. "We're all in the backyard."

Thomas let go of his mom's hand and snagged mine. "Want to see my dinosaurs, Artie?"

I glanced at Kate, who nodded her okay. "Heck, yeah, I do. Which is your favorite?"

"T-rex!" he said. "But have you heard of a velociraptor?"

"I'm not sure," I said, tapping my chin. "Can you tell me about it?"

And off he went, talking about four-inch claws and excellent eyesight and did I know that some dinosaurs had feathers?

By the time he'd finished his explanation, we'd made it into the backyard, and I glanced up from the gorgeous blue-eyed cherub to see a sea of people staring her me. "Um, hi?" I said and waved.

Pierce's mom came out of a door, a huge grin on her face. "I'm so happy you made it to dinner!" She crossed over to me, arms extended, and I found myself swept into one of those quintessential mom hugs—warm and tight that felt like she would hold on to me for as long as I needed to be held.

There was nothing like mom hugs.

"Hi," she said, dropping her arms when I leaned back slightly.

"Hi," I murmured, clearing my tight throat. "I don't know your name."

She laughed. "Dorinne. But my friends call me Dory."

"Are we friends?" I asked, stepping back.

Another laugh. "I hope so."

"Me, too," I said, and though I'd been reticent to accept the invite in the first place, I couldn't say I disliked the thought that I might have made a friend in Dory.

"I'm Dave," a man said as Dorinne shifted to the side. He stuck out a hand. "I'm—"

"Pierce's dad," I exclaimed, looking between him and Pierce. The resemblance was uncanny—same blue-gray eyes, same nose, same jaw, same broad shoulders and lean hips. The only difference was that his brown hair had a few gray strands mixed in.

Smiles erupted all around, including on Pierce's face.

"I'm definitely a Daniels," he said. "That's for sure."

"No milkman's babies in this family," another tall, statuesque blonde said, this one with a baby on her hip. "I'm Marie, by the way. Four of the terrors are mine, along with that male terror"—a man with brown hair and eyes waved, said "I'm Joe."—"I'm Pierce's sister."

"Much older," Pierce chimed in.

I plunked my hands onto my hips. "That's rude."

"Marie, meet Artie. She's also *much older* than me," he teased. "I still think she's okay."

"Seriously?" My foot started tapping. "Let's not forget the fact that I'm *fifteen* years older than you."

"And don't look a day over fourteen."

I glared.

He grinned, totally unremorseful. "Remember what I said about teasing in this family?"

"Remember what I said about my talent for sticking cameras up into places they don't belong?"

"Remember when I said I like it when you threaten me?"

I lifted a brow. "I don't recall that particular conversation."

"Hmm." His lips twitched. "Well, I guess I was remiss in telling you."

I shook my head.

Dorinne cleared her throat, drawing my attention back to her, and I tried not to notice the knowing expression on her face. The distance thing was getting harder to remember when it was just so much damn fun talking to Pierce.

His family wasn't bad either.

"What's in the bag?" Marie asked.

"Wine," Pierce answered, opening the bag enough to reveal the contents.

"Oh, yes," Marie said, clapping her hands together. "You're now officially my favorite person in the history of all people."

My lips curved. "Well, you're my kind of person."

"Cheap date?" Marie said with a smirk.

"She means, an alcoholic," Pierce quipped.

Marie huffed, and I poked him in the ribs. "I meant smart," I announced. "Knows a good thing when she sees it."

"I'd just like it stated for the record that *that's* a Daniels family trait," Pierce murmured, close enough to my ear that I shivered. "We see good things and we go for them."

I remembered.

Too freaking well.

"Holster the smolder," I muttered.

He chuckled but stepped away, taking the wine with him. "Be right back."

"Chill the champagne!" I called.

"On it."

"Champagne?" Marie asked.

"Seemed like maybe you guys might want to celebrate everyone being together," I said with a shrug. "If no one's a fan, I'll take it home with me."

"Oh, we're fans," Kate told her. "And I concur with Marie. You're good people, Artemis."

"Artie," I corrected. "Artemis is just . . ." I shook my head. "A little to extra, even for me."

"Artie's not a boy's name," Thomas announced, running over with a dinosaur in his hand. He held it up to me for an examination, which I dutifully completed, making sure to take the task seriously.

"I see those long claws you were talking about," I said, carefully handing it back.

Thomas grinned and ran off.

"Come on." Marie slipped her arm through mine, leading me over to a large table that was set up on the back porch. It provided a bird's eye view of the kids running around on the lawn. "They're a little pent-up after the flight."

"I can imagine," I said, sitting down in a chair and surveying them. "Those Daniels genes are strong, huh?" I don't think I'd ever seen a group of kids and adults who looked so similar, even despite Pierce and his dad having brown hair and gray eyes as opposed to the blond hair and blues of the rest of the bunch, they were still obviously Daniels. The only oddballs were me and the husbands. But it seemed that their DNA had been overcome by the pure dominance of the Daniels'.

Kate laughed. "You could say that." She pointed at a little blonde girl toddling after the rest. "She's the only one without blue eyes. Hank likes to joke that I messed up with her."

"Either that," a man said, coming over and kissing the top of her head, "or my DNA finally prevailed. Hi"—he waved—"I'm the previously mentioned Hank."

I laughed. "Hi, previously mentioned Hank."

Kate rolled her eyes. "Sit, Hank. Plus, it's not dominance if fate is just finally throwing us a bone."

"Dominance or fate," Joe said, "I'm still waiting for my bone."

"There's a comment there," Marie chimed in. "But because Artie is new, I'm going to give her a break."

I grinned. "Obliged."

And cue silence.

I opened my mouth, readying to ask about their travel day, or to make a joke, anything to keep the conversation going. It was a skill I'd acquired over the years, a way for me to keep everyone included.

I'd never felt the need with Pierce.

Our conversations, our blips of quiet had been comfortable from day one.

I supposed it wouldn't necessarily cross over to his entire family.

Except, I got as far as opening my mouth before Kate said, "You're really good with Thomas. He's usually so shy."

I should have known the Daniels hoard would be able to carry a conversation.

"He's adorable," I agreed. "They all are."

Kate smiled. "I think so, too. Of course, I'm biased." A beat. "Do you have any of your own?"

"Oh, no," I said. "I like kids, always thought I would have some one day, but I never . . ." I shrugged off the wave of longing. "Well, anyway, I think I've worked my way through those prime reproductive years and now it's too late."

"No," Marie said. "What are you? Thirty-three? Thirty-four?"

"Forty-two." I laughed at their shocked expressions. "I wasn't kidding about the whole fifteen years older thing."

"Wow," Kate said. "I need your beauty care routine."

My lips twitched. "I think most of it comes from not having to wrangle a bunch like that."

The table laughed.

"Katie's right though," Hank said once they'd stopped. "Tom doesn't really talk to strangers much. He must have seen something special in you."

I bit my lip.

Marie outright snorted.

Pierce came and sat at the table, "I think you've been watching too much *Sesame Street*."

Hank threw up his hands. "You guys are terrible. I'm trying to give the woman a compliment."

"I'd rather hear how it was to work with Zane Potter," Kate said. "Is he as gorgeous in person as he is in the movies?" The sigh that followed her question was a typical response to the sexy-as-sin A-lister.

Pierce made a disgusted noise, one that was echoed by the husbands.

That too was typical from the non-fawning men and partners of the Zane Potter fan club.

"It really should be illegal how beautiful the man is," I said.

"I knew it!" Marie said.

"But he's also a really nice guy," I went on. "It's almost sickening that someone should be both so pretty and so lovely on the inside."

"Ooh." Kate squealed. "I'm so glad my crush can live on."

"Okay, so now that it's well-established our love of all things Zane Potter can continue, I want to know which of your films is your favorite," Marie said.

The hardest question to answer. And also the easiest.

"Which of your kids is your favorite?" I countered.

"Chase," she said without missing a beat. "He doesn't talk back yet."

More laughter, more smiles, more of Pierce just sitting next to me as the conversation flowed, as the teasing and chuckles continued. It was easy and effortless, as though I'd known these people my whole life.

Look, I knew I could charm people, could carry a conversation, and make it so that everyone in a group had a great time. The difference was that with this group, I didn't have to. I was included and peppered with questions as often as I sat back and enjoyed the banter. Everyone got a turn, everyone dished it back in response. I was called out on my apparently egregious use of Dory's special ketchup on her delicious meatloaf—which was some voodoo mystery magic with brown sugar and yellow mustard and ketchup that I could have taken home in a Tupperware and eaten by the spoonful—but then the teasing moved on to Kate and her hogging of the butter.

It was some sort of strange, delightful universe into which I'd descended.

And I wasn't sure I wanted to be lifted back out.

I certainly didn't want to leave when the sun set and the kiddos and their parents began yawning then eventually drifted off to bed. I didn't want to leave after Dorinne gave me another hug and Jack a pat on the shoulder before they too cried off for sleep, being still on East Coast time.

I didn't want to leave as Pierce sat quietly next to me, both of our gazes on the lights in the distance.

Nor when he got up and returned with the final bottle of wine, refilling my glass.

And I didn't want to leave when he laced our fingers together as the sounds of the quieting house descended around us.

I wasn't sure I *ever* wanted to leave.

But I finished my glass of wine and I went anyway.

TEN

Pierce

I AWOKE to the sound of a baby crying, the smell of bacon permeating the closed door.

Groaning, I rolled over and glanced at my cell.

Just after five in the morning, after having been up until almost one.

But I wasn't irritated.

Rather, I got out of bed with a smile, happy that my family was there and that the house I'd bought anticipating their visits was finally full.

I showered, threw on a pair of sweats, then walked down the hall and into the kitchen. The crew was gathered around the big table that took up one wall. I could honestly say this was the first time every chair had been occupied, some of them double as the kiddos seated themselves on the adults' laps.

"Morning, honey," my mom said, waving a spatula from her place at the stove.

My dad grunted, face buried behind a paper, and Grayson greeted me with his typical full-speed hug and go. Thomas and the twins were occupied with pancakes, my sisters with feeding the littlest ones. Hank was stirring eggs on the stove. Joe feeding toast into the toaster.

I'd been fully invaded.

And it was awesome.

Seeing that adult pancakes were imminent, I pulled out some plates and silverware, bringing both over to the table.

"You furnished a playroom?" Marie asked the moment my ass hit the seat.

I shrugged, reached for the carafe and poured myself some coffee. "Had to give them something to do while they were here."

"Same as the playground?"

"Weather's nice. Might as well take advantage of it."

Her eyes narrowed. "You didn't have—"

"I *wanted* to."

"You—"

"Enough," my dad said, gruffly, not a morning person, whether on West Coast or East Coast time. "Pierce has the money. He wanted to take care of the kids. Shut up and be gracious about it."

Marie's face went comically blank for a heartbeat before she sighed. "You're the little brother," she said. "We're supposed to take care of you."

"It's a man—"

"You'd better not finish that statement with *thing*, Dad," Kate chimed in, wrestling a spoon from Gabriella before she could launch it across the room.

"What?" He let the paper fall to reveal his face. "It's not a surprise that a Daniels man would want to take care of his family."

Marie narrowed her eyes, and I made the conscious decision to defuse the fight.

Yes, I did think my father had a point. This was my family. I'd bleed for them without a second thought, do without so they could have everything they needed. But I also knew what my sisters were thinking.

Our family was a unit.

We closed ranks. We looked after each other. We were Daniels.

That meant something, too.

"How about we all just keep taking care of each other?"

Marie's gaze flicked between me, my dad, and Kate before she sighed. "Yes," she said. "Let's keep doing that. Except some of us don't have unlimited income to keep our nieces and nephews in toys."

Ah.

That was what this was about.

"You already flew us out," she grumbled. "Now this and what I'm assuming are going to be extravagant presents for everyone. We can't give that back, Pierce."

"First of all, I don't need it back. Everything I've given is because I have the means and I *want* to."

"It's too much—"

I reached across the table, rested my hand on Katie's. "I seem to remember someone sending me care packages when I first moved to L.A." I turned to Marie. "Money being mysteriously deposited into my account when I was almost ready to give up on my dream." I wrapped my fingers around my coffee cup. "I also remember everyone flying out for my first premiere, even though it was for that crappy indie film."

Silence.

Then, "Damn, Pierce, you're good," Joe said.

Everyone laughed, the seriousness of the moment broken. Katie grinned at him. "So, you're saying we should just shut up and accept it gracefully?"

"Yes, that." I set my arm on the back of Marie's chair. "You think you're capable of that?"

A snort. "I don't think graceful is in my vocabulary."

My mom carried a plate of bacon to the table, Hank trailing her with pancakes and eggs, Joe with toast. Kiddos' bottoms were shifted as the adults found their seats and for a few minutes, there weren't any arguments. Rather, plates were passed around, syrup and butter were spread liberally onto delicious circles of carbs, and bacon was consumed.

It was the usual Daniels chaos.

But it was home.

And Marie stopped giving me shit about the stuff I'd bought for the kids.

I knew that would change when we opened presents in a few days time. Yes, I'd gone overboard. No, I wasn't done, especially now that I'd decided to send them all on a vacation.

I thought that I might be able to swing some time off from filming in Turks and Caicos and there was a fabulous all-inclusive resort there, complete with a water park and even a swim-up bar for the kids that served fancy smoothies, and childcare so the adults could have some alone time. I was planning on sending an email that morning to Shelby to arrange the details.

So, yeah, Marie flipping out again was pretty much guaranteed.

It was also pretty much par for the course.

My mom was the first to break the non-food conversation, and she did it with a bang that my oldest sister should be proud of, setting her fork down and fixing me with the OG stare that had never failed to get one of us kids to spill our guts.

"So, Pierce, how long have you been in love with Artemis?"

A bomb might as well have gone off in that kitchen.

A figurative one anyway. Kate dropped her fork, Marie's jaw fell open, Dad's paper slipped from limp fingers, Joe's eyes were practically lost in his hairline, a half-chewed bite of toast fell from Hank's mouth.

Even the kids went quiet.

"Umm . . ."

What the fuck could I possibly say to that?

"I'm not in love with her, Mom."

My dad rolled his eyes. "Bull sh—" Marie coughed. "*Pucky.* Any idiot could see that you're head over heels for her."

"We're business associates, nothing more."

Lie.

I thought of the way we'd sat on the back porch the night before, fingers laced together, words coming infrequent and quiet, but the silence that had stretched in between wasn't awkward. It was . . . another form of home.

"Man," Hank said. "You know I usually have your back, since we guys have to stick together in this family." He ignored the scoff from Kate. "But even I can say with certainty that you've got it bad for her."

"You like her," Kate said softly.

"Of course, I do," I replied. "She's brilliant and beautiful. We always have fun together."

"It's more than fun," my mom murmured.

I knew what she was getting at. The undeniable spark that Artie and I had. We were like two planets revolving around a sun, on our own trajectories unless we were close. Then we fucked with astronomy and created our own orbits.

Around each other.

It's why we always found each other at events.

Why working together was proving to be effortless.

Why sleeping with her had changed me. Permanently. But—

"It's not the same for her," I said, picking up my fork and shoving a bite of now-tasteless pancakes into my mouth.

Marie nudged my shoulder. "If that's true, then why does she look at you like you hung the moon?"

I shook my head. "It's not like that with us."

"Because of you? Or because of her?"

What had I been thinking about loving that my family was home? Because I was quickly rethinking that sentiment. They didn't understand, didn't know that even though I liked Artie, she would never let me close enough to bridge that distance she kept between herself and the rest of the world.

"I'm too young—"

"Nope." Kate rolled her eyes. "Nice try, but if that really bothered her, she wouldn't be able to joke so effortlessly about it."

"She's scared of commitment."

"*That* maybe is true," my mom said. "But it's also not the entire story."

I shot to my feet, crossed to the sink, and plunked my plate inside, whipping back to face them with crossed arms. "She won't let me get close enough to love her."

"If she's worth it, you find a way," Joe murmured, smiling over at his wife with softness in his eyes.

"And . . . that's to say, I . . . she—*I*—" I dropped my chin to my chest, words shuddering to a stop as I realized just what I was feeling.

"I'm scared," I said on a sigh.

My dad dropped his hand onto my shoulder, squeezed lightly. "Bingo."

"It's always easy to find the reasons to stay away, to keep your heart safe," Marie murmured. "But when you finally find the courage to leap, to grab on to the possibility of something special, it's worth all that terror."

"Ringing endorsement," I muttered.

Marie laughed, coming over to hug me. "Come on, it's not so bad," she said. "We're here. We'll help."

May the film gods save me.

"Mare," Joe warned.

My mom clapped her hands together. "Yes! We'll all work together, and we'll find a way to get you guys together."

"Either that, or we'll get you fired," Hank joked.

Six sets of adult eyes—and a few young ones—glared his way.

"What?" he asked on a shrug. "Too soon?"

Kate walked over and smacked him on the arm. "Too soon, you pain in the butt." Hank countered this by tugging her down into his lap and kissing her . . . then started tickling. My sister shrieked, squirming for several moments before he relented . . . and then kissed *him*.

Teasing. Tickling. Persistence.

It had won the most armored Daniels' heart.

But could it have a chance at winning one that had been wounded and sliced to shreds, one that had needed to be rebuilt with steel and rebar in order to survive?

For the first time in nearly six years, I thought I finally had the courage to find out.

ELEVEN

Artie

THERE WAS a woman on my doorstep.

With a child clinging to her hand, and Pierce was standing just a couple feet behind her. "Hey," he said, with a short wave. "We're just on our way out, but I wanted to drop by those photos I'd mentioned."

Brows drawing down, I obediently stepped back, allowing Kate, Thomas, and Pierce to come through into the entrance of my house.

His eyes met mine and I shivered, remembering what we'd done the last time he'd been in my home.

"Fixed that table," he murmured.

My lips parted, a rush of air slipping through. Then I stuffed the urge to launch myself into his arms deep down—his sister and nephew were there for fuck's sake. "New one," I said, keeping my tone light as I blabbered. "I redecorated last year. New kitchen, new floors. The only place I didn't touch was my bedroom."

His eyes went hot.

Shit. That was a miscalculation, mentioning the whole ed-bay-oom-ray thing.

Last night had changed things between us. Hell, who was I kidding? It had *always* been different with Pierce than other men for me. I'd just been able to run and avoid, to pretend he was just the same as anyone else. But he *was* different. It was why I'd broken a rule by sleeping with him in the first place, why I'd looked out for him in the years since. Why I couldn't stay away when I saw him.

Friends.

I'd really just wanted it to be that.

Unfortunately, I didn't think that was where things would end up with us.

And that was absolutely terrifying.

I just didn't know what was more frightening—losing the small snippets of him I'd allowed into my life because I couldn't be what he deserved or finding the strength to let down my barriers and allow him in.

It was why I lived my life in temporaries.

I just didn't think I could live in temporaries with Pierce.

Where once I was able to ignore the draw, or at the very least smother the urge to leap into his arms, now I was on the struggle bus. Big time. Meeting his family, sitting with him on the porch, not needing to fill the silence, not having to be on or charming or funny. After my family had imploded, after my mom had died, I'd made sure to only need me.

And I wasn't sure I'd ever had *that*.

A family that loved and cared and didn't hurt—physically or emotionally. Sisters who teased and lifted up in equal turns, a dad who was quiet but steady and kind. A mom who was . . . strong enough to not allow someone to hurt her.

If I'd grown up in Pierce's family—

"Your house is beautiful," Kate exclaimed, pulling me from

my thoughts. "And these floors are absolutely gorgeous. Was it a pain to have them redone? Hank and I are considering it."

"Honestly?" I asked.

Kate nodded.

"I ended up staying in a hotel for a week," I said, lips quirking. "I travel so much for work, but for some idiotic reason, I decided that I needed to be home to make sure they were doing it right."

Pierce snorted.

"I know, I know," I said. "My control freak tendencies are strong. But it backfired, because the one week I was home that month, I didn't even get to sleep in my own bed."

Kate laughed then bent to stroke her fingers across the wide, hand-scraped, gray plank. "Well, hotel or not, it was well worth it."

"True," I said, then swept a hand toward my kitchen. "Can I get you guys something to drink? A popsicle for Thomas?"

Thomas's eyes perked up, and he nodded jerkily from his position at his mom's side. "I think that's a yes," Kate said, smiling. "I'd love a water, too, if you don't mind, Artie. Corralling these boys is hard work."

Thomas nodded again. "I'm a terror," he announced proudly.

"Well," I said, smothering a laugh at his child honesty, "Mr. Terror, do you want to walk with me so you can pick out your popsicle?" I asked. "I also don't think you finished telling me about T-rexes."

He considered that. "Okay," he said, and he walked over to take my hand, his shyness of being in a new place fading in the face of popsicles and dinosaur talk.

"Did you know that T-rexes had really bad breath?"

I shook my head solemnly. "No, I did not know that," I said, leading us into the kitchen and opening up the freezer.

Thomas's eyes widened.

Pierce whistled.

"I have an unhealthy obsession with popsicles," I said, feeling suddenly self-conscious. It was the truth, though. I love them. The sugarier and more dye-filled, the better.

"I wish I could eat those and have an ass like yours," Kate said enviously.

"The key is not caring what your ass looks like," I said, then made a face, adding in a teasing tone. "Well, that and not having kids."

She laughed, went along with my joke. "That's true. They do ruin everything."

I held up a box of popsicles. "So what's your poison? Strawberry? Cherry? Grape? Or will you live on the edge and go for green apple?"

Kate hesitated then shrugged. "Why not? I'll take strawberry."

I handed her strawberry. "Thomas?"

"Cherry!"

I handed him cherry.

"Pierce?"

Silence.

I glanced up at him, saw that the smolder from almost six years before had made a reappearance. My mouth went dry, my thighs trembled, and—

"Here, honey, come over to the sink so I can help you with the wrapper," Kate murmured, and my gaze flew to her and Thomas walking away from the freezer.

"Strawberry."

I gulped.

How in the hell had the man made that sound sexy?

Oh, probably because he was burning me to cinders with his gaze.

I reached into the box, pulling out a strawberry popsicle and holding it out. Pierce took it, but slowly, his fingers drifting down the inside of my wrist and making me shiver.

"Thanks, sweetheart."

Another shiver, barely able to nod at Kate when she asked if it was okay to take Thomas onto the back porch, so he didn't drip on the floor.

Pierce was close.

Near enough that I could scent him, and that paired with him being in my house, just inches from me, so close that all my senses—touch, smell, taste, sight, hearing—were all on high alert, made my brain haze over.

My fingertips ached to run over his chest, to explore the abs I'd spent an evening kissing my way across.

My nose was filled with the spicy maleness of his scent.

My ears were filled with the pounding of my heartbeat.

My eyes traced up and down his body, reminding my mind how good it had been to be in his arms, to cuddle close and be held like I was important.

My mouth watered to taste his.

I licked my lips. Pierce's head dropped so I could feel his hot breath puffing against them.

His vulnerability at the awards ceremony the previous year had lifted the bandage covering my need for him, had made me yearn to see him happy and fulfilled, even if it wasn't with me.

The past nine months of planning the film had nudged that Band-Aid further, had made me wish when he found his happy and content it *could* be me, even while knowing that was impossible.

Scotland had prodded the bandage even more, over-whelming me with yearning, all while knowing it could not be.

And last night . . .

Well, last night, the bandage had disappeared.

I was flayed open and vulnerable. I wanted him, wanted more of how he made me feel special and included, more of his wonderful, teasing family.

It could not be.

Sighing and wondering why the mental statement gave me all sorts of Gandalf the Gray vibes from *Lord of the Rings* ("*You shall not pass!*"), I pushed the memory of my night with Pierce from my mind.

He was here for pictures. That was it.

But then he cupped my cheek, murmured, "Artie."

I reached into the box, grabbed a popsicle at random, and whipped around to shove the remaining ice pops back in the freezer. It took me several tries to shove the box back in and close the door, probably crumpling it to hell and breaking them into tiny unsatisfying pieces, but in the end, I did manage to stow everything safely in the freezer.

Too bad *I* couldn't fit.

If so, I could avoid what was coming next.

"She's right."

My forehead was resting against the cool metal when I asked, "Who's right?"

"Kate."

I tilted my head to the side, peered back at him over my shoulder. He'd returned to leaning back against the island, one ankle crossed over the other. I turned so my forehead was against the cool metal of the fridge again and asked, "About what?"

"Your ass *is* fantastic."

Heat. One minute I was feeling totally fine—okay, lie, because I was definitely off-kilter. But one second, I was pulling the strands of my self-control together, shoring up my spine to do the right thing, and the next I was in flames. Desire pooled in my stomach, spreading out to my limbs, making my fingers tremble and almost dropping the popsicle, right along with my restraint.

Pierce recognized that and took the former from me, setting both of them on the counter before coming back and standing very close. His front was a hairsbreadth away from my spine, the heat radiating off him and seeping through the cotton of my shirt, warming my skin.

I spun to face him.

My willpower at resisting him was shredded simply by that proximity, by the way he stared down at me.

Need reflected back.

And softness.

That was the most dangerous. The softness.

I shook my head, attempting to clear it. "We can't—"

"Tell me you don't feel it," he murmured, running his fingers lightly down my cheek, along my jaw. "Tell me you haven't spent the last six years fighting whatever draw there is between us."

"Pierce—" I shook my head again. "We *shouldn't*—"

"Shouldn't keep ignoring it," he said, head dropping, lips trailing along the same path. "In *that*, I am in complete agreement."

Gooseflesh erupted on my arms, my nape.

My hand lifted, to push him away, to tug him nearer. I wasn't sure. "T-that's not what I meant. Things are too complicated—"

"Because of the movie?" he asked, and I nodded, panic curling in my insides, desperation building, and out-pacing desire for the moment. I took a step forward, forcing Pierce to take a step back or our bodies would collide.

I wasn't sure which option I wanted.

Fuck, who was I kidding? My body *wanted* to be pressed to his. It was my brain that was having a hard time keeping up.

The organ took the opportunity to grab on to any excuse to stop this before it went too far. "We can't jeopardize the movie. It's too important to both of us, and if we act on this and it goes wrong . . ."

We hadn't crossed that point of no return.

If we did—

"You told me you wouldn't be around much for actual filming," he said, and my gut sank, remembering the conversation we'd had a few nights after I'd fled Scotland. It wasn't like I planned to just drop everything to do with the project, but a lot of my initial legwork was done. I could review the dailies from anywhere, and God knew I had plenty of other work to fill the rest of my time. I'd used that excuse to create distance and . . .

Well, it was backfiring now, since he was using my reasoning against me.

Smart man. Infuriating man.

He settled his hands on my shoulders, massaging lightly. "This seems like as good a time as any to see what we could be, sweetheart," he murmured. "We'll have some time together, but it'll be limited because we're both going to our separate locations, because our work hours will be long and intense. So that time will be tempered, by the distance *and* the hours. It'll force us to take things slow, to get to know each other."

I shook my head.

Not because I necessarily thought he was wrong. Mostly, I shook it because I was trying to knock the argument from my mind. He was making sense, being reasonable . . .

And, *fuck*, I liked him.

I'd never liked a man this much before.

Never felt this connection or yearning or—he shifted so his hips brushed lightly against mine, making my nerves explode with sensation—*temptation*.

Yes. That was the word.

I lived my life in temporaries because I'd lived through my permanence being torn to shreds. I knew that stability could be a false façade, that everything could be ripped away in a moment's notice.

Temporary was safe.

I didn't get attached, and I could leave when things got dicey.

I wouldn't get hurt.

Pierce could hurt me. He could absolutely devastate me. Just the thought of giving in and then losing him in the end was absolutely terrifying.

I couldn't—I couldn't do this, risk everything . . . I just *couldn't*.

TWELVE

Pierce

SHE WAS GOING to say no.

Of course, she was.

This was too much too soon.

The plan was to have Kate and Thomas come with me to deliver the pictures I could have easily emailed, to use Thomas's utter adorableness to convince Artie to come to Disneyland with us. To sugar her up, coax her on a few rides, get her out on a date that she didn't realize was a date.

But then I'd gotten close.

And I'd not played it cool.

Marie was going to smack me around.

My internal dialogue wasn't serious, of course, but the words still clued me in, as though a hand had struck my brain. Smack. Me. Around.

Fuck.

I got it.

I knew the story. Everyone in this town did. Artie's mom

and dad, Ben and Tawny Miller, had been B-list celebrities, stars of several failed sitcoms, one successful soap, and had raised Artie in the film world. That wasn't particularly uncommon in L.A. Neither was the fact that Ben had been abusive to Tawny—and apparently to Artie as well, though that wasn't common knowledge in any narrative I'd ever heard. The salacious and gossip-inducing part came when Artie's dad had been caught by the paparazzi, punching and kicking her mom, leaving Tawny bruised and bloodied and surrounded by camera flashes before fleeing in their car.

He'd somehow avoided arrest and made it over the border to Canada.

That was just one shitty piece of the whole horrible scenario, because life had gotten worse for Artie. First, her mom had begun mailing cash to her husband, supplying Ben with enough money to live comfortably north of the border, even at the expense of Artie's and her own well-being.

Then Tawny had packed up their house, sold their belongings, and followed Artie's dad to Canada.

Story had it that Ben would have continued to avoid detection if he hadn't gotten cocky and attempted to attend a fan event for the soap, needing or wanting the attention, and drawing altogether too much of the wrong sort from the Washington State Patrol when he'd been joyriding on his way home.

He'd been picked up, booked, and shipped back to California to face prosecution by the District Attorney.

With Tawny at his side.

Along with Artie being dragged back into the drama.

So, no wonder she was gun shy about possibly pursuing a relationship. She needed to be coaxed, gentled, tugged along.

Not hit over the head with my desire.

Fuck.

She shook her head. "I'm—"

"It's okay," I murmured, knowing I needed to employ a tactical retreat, to not push too hard so I could coax on another day. "I understand, sweetheart." I placed the pretty much useless flash drive on the counter next to the popsicles. "I'll go—"

Her hand on my arm stopped me.

"No."

If this had been one of my films, the camera would have focused on her fingers circling my bicep, the slight sheen on her pale pink nails glittering in the overhead lights, the clunky gold ring she wore on her thumb sparkling, then it would have cut to my face, captured my jaw tightening, my eyes widening with hope, the way my breath froze on my lips.

Slowly, it would have panned back to frame us both.

The way my body rotated toward hers, how she drifted closer, that hand sliding up to rest on my shoulder. And I sure as shit would have caught the shudder wracking her frame, the way we subconsciously leaned toward each other.

"You say you know," she said, chin dropping forward so it rested on her chest. "But how could you possibly?"

I didn't reply, instinct telling me that my words weren't needed at that moment.

Hers were the ones that mattered.

She glanced up, and every muscle in my body locked.

"No one—" A shake of her head. "That's not fair," she murmured. "Plenty of other people have endured worse abuse than I went through. Perhaps not on such a public scale, but aside from the fact that my pain was tabloid fodder, my story isn't that unique."

"It's yours," I said. "And your pain isn't discounted just because someone else might have suffered more. You're allowed to be hurt. You're allowed to have whatever feelings about your past that you do, and you don't have to justify them to me or the world." I covered her hand with mine. "You answer to yourself, Artie. Not me. Not the press. Not the world."

She huffed out a breath, dropped her forehead to my shoulder. "Several of my financers would strongly disagree with you."

I chuckled. "Probably. But you also know that I'm talking emotions, not electronic funds transfers."

Her lips moved against my shirt. "For some of them, that's one and the same."

"True." My fingers wove into her ponytail, slid gently through the silky strands as we stood there, her barriers not quite down enough for me to feel comfortable yanking her against my chest and slamming my mouth down on hers, caveman style. But the barriers had retracted a hairsbreadth, and so I just stayed in place, stroking her hair, letting her know I was there, I was listening.

"If you know the story," she murmured, "then you probably know all the gory public versions. The video of the beating circulated widely on news outlets." Her eyes came up to meet mine. "Did you know someone put it on YouTube right before the premiere of *Last Night Out*? Lucky me, it got one hundred and sixty million views before YouTube pulled it down."

Fucking people.

She shook her head. "If one of our trailers had gotten that many, I'd be thrilled." A sigh. "A video about my painful past? Not ideal."

"Artie."

Her fingers squeezed lightly on my shoulder. "Just let me finish, okay?"

I clenched my jaw, shut the fuck up, and nodded.

"I didn't change my name because my face was out there,

because I knew I couldn't hide from my past, that it would always creep in and find me." She swallowed. "I had already been in some film and television roles while my parents were working, and after my dad went to jail, I had to keep taking them. Mostly because my mom was all but blacklisted and if I hadn't taken them, her job at the department store wouldn't have been enough for us to live on." She shook her head. "But those producers and directors didn't want *me*. They wanted the sad, beautiful little girl to help propel their story or show into the news."

"That's fucked up."

"It's the business," she said. "It's my life. It's why I can be successful and still have tabloid articles written about my parents. It's why my mom committing suicide was a top news story, why those clips are constantly put up on YouTube. It's painful and horrible and . . . it's my life."

From my limited experience as a white male director, I understood how vicious this life could be, but I guess what I didn't understand was why she didn't just leave it all behind.

Her free hand covered mine at the back of her head, loosening it from the strands as she put some distance between us.

Distance I really fucking hated.

"I've seen that look before," she murmured. "You're wondering why I didn't just sell anything of value and get the fuck out of Hollywood when I turned eighteen." Her thumb brushed across my knuckles. "It's all I know, Pierce. But more than that, it's what I love."

I sucked in a breath, released it slowly. "And you're really good at it."

Artie's smile hit me right in the gut. "Of course, I am."

"And modest, too," I teased.

"Yup," she agreed, before her smile faded. "You need to know that I did leave the life for a few years, right after my mom died. My dad had just gotten out of prison, my mom was gone. I couldn't take a reality where she wasn't around, but he was."

"Doesn't it make you mad that she—" I cut myself off, realizing that wasn't a fair question to ask when Artie clearly cared about her mother.

"That she killed herself? Or that she uprooted my life to stay with my abusive father?" Her thumb continued its tracing. "Ask your questions, Pierce. God knows, I've been in this city long enough to have been asked *everything*. Yes, I was furious that she killed herself and left me alone with my father. Yes, I thought she was weak for a long time—both for that and for staying with my dad."

Her eyes filled with tears that she blinked back. "But you can't judge another person on your standards. Did I want her to hit him back? To turn him into the police? To take us both back home and make a new life for us that was something we could be proud of? Of course, I did." Her lips flattened out for a long moment. "But she couldn't be what I needed. She was a lot of very wonderful things as a mother, but she couldn't be strong or assertive or protect me from the monsters in my life."

Fuck it.

I couldn't stand there and see Artie in pain and not touch her, not comfort her. Gently, I wrapped my arms around her and pulled her against me. "I'm so sorry, sweetheart," I murmured, stroking my hand down her spine.

She didn't reply.

But she also didn't push out of my hold, just stayed there and let me keep her near. Eventually, though, she leaned back enough to ask, "Now, do you understand why this between us isn't a good idea?"

I'd been patient.

I'd been understanding.

I'd been thoughtful and caring.

But now, I was infuriated.

"No," I snapped. "Fucking *no*, I don't understand why this isn't a good idea. Because yes, your childhood was shit, but fuck, Artie, that wasn't on you. Your parents aren't you. You're not the same as your mother. You're sure as shit not your father. This isn't about them, it's about us." I blew out a breath, trying to calm my tone, but how she could so calmly shoulder the burden of her past, one she had no bearing on creating, was way beyond my pay grade. "This is bullshit."

Okay, so not much calmer.

Her eyes filled with fire and she pulled out of my hold. "It's not—"

"I let you talk," I said firmly, taking a step closer. "Now, it's my turn. This—*us*—isn't about whatever fucked up shit your parents had going on. This isn't about how *my* parents have had a rock-steady relationship. Because what is between us is about *us* and how we feel and how we make each other feel. Anything else is just background noise."

"That's naïve," she said, pacing away.

I didn't miss the fact that she'd deliberately put the kitchen island between us.

Barriers.

Not just because she was locked down, but also because there was some part of her that was still scared of what a man could do to her.

That sobered me more than anything else could.

"The outside world factors in," she said. "We don't live in a bubble. The past, the present, your family, our colleagues all play a part."

I forced myself to lean against the counter instead of going to her. "I'm not saying that we live in a vacuum, but the first and the most important thing in a relationship is what two people have between each other." I gentled my voice. "And what we have is special. It's worth not just throwing that away."

She rolled her eyes. "Fairy tales don't exist, Pierce."

"Maybe not, but happily ever afters do."

And with those famous last words, I succeeded in driving Artie from the room.

Who said romance was dead?

THIRTEEN

Artie

I MADE it as far as the hall before my fury got the better of me.

Whipping around, I strode back into the kitchen.

Then promptly ran into Pierce, whose gray eyes had darkened, warning of a storm on the horizon.

I stopped. Glared.

"You really piss me off, did you know that?"

He opened his mouth to reply, but I didn't let him get any words out. I launched myself at him, wrapping my legs around his hips, my arms around his shoulders, and slammed my lips down onto his.

There wasn't an ounce of hesitation or delay. One second, I was snapping a question at him, the next, his tongue was in my mouth, his hands cupping my ass.

This was six years of pent-up need, six years of one night not being enough and yet me kidding myself that it was. This was six years of me hiding and pretending and trying to force a square peg into a round hole.

I couldn't be just friends with Pierce.

That option had gone out the window the moment I'd dragged him back to my car all those years ago.

He nipped my bottom lip, making me gasp and jerk. "Pay attention," he growled and then nipped and kissed and licked his way across my jaw, down my throat. Heat, always banked but at the ready when he was near, exploded through my body. Liquid pooled between my thighs, desire made my fingers, clenched so tightly on his shoulders, tremble.

One movement spun us, flipping us so my back was to the wall and all the lovely hard lines of Pierce were pressing into me.

Hard cock between my thighs.

Hard stomach against mine.

Hard chest brushing my breasts.

Fuck, but I wanted him.

He kissed the spot where my throat met my shoulder, then sucked hard enough to leave a mark. Thirty years since I'd had my first hickey and I never would have thought they were still sexy.

Pierce leaving a mark, however?

Yeah, that was fucking hot.

Then he was back kissing me, mouth plundering mine as his tongue slipped between my lips to dance with mine, teeth finding my bottom lip and biting just hard enough to sting before his tongue soothed the spot.

Distantly, I felt us moving, knew we'd left the wall, but the rest of my brain was focused on what I was feeling, what he was doing to my body.

A change of motion, gravity re-exerting its pull, and I found my back on something soft. My bedroom, I recognized through the haze, but then Pierce's hands were at the button on my jeans, flicking it open and sliding the zipper down. Hands at my ankles, tugging at the stiff material, tossing it to the floor, along with my socks. Warm palms sliding up over my shins, my thighs, one moving in to cup me through the cotton of my underwear.

Not lace.

Not sexy.

His eyes told me he didn't give two shits.

I reached for the hem of his shirt, yanking it up to his armpits as I struggled to get it over his head. He only let me fight with it for a couple of seconds before batting my hands away and ripping it off to send it in the general direction of my jeans.

"Fuck, I've missed these," I murmured, running a finger across his abs, pussy aching with the need to get my mouth there.

"Later," he gritted, snagging my hands and placing them above my head.

A second later, my T-shirt was gone, my bra quickly following suit.

Which was the moment I realized I'd snapped something in Pierce, some form of control, some typically gentle part of his personality.

Gentle was gone.

A tempest was in its place.

My bra had disappeared before I finished the thought, his mouth descending, dragging along my throat, down between my breasts. Then, without warning, he sucked a nipple into his mouth, making me cry out and arch off the mattress. His tongue flicked. The suction was intense and unforgiving, but it was also exactly what I needed, the final movement that snapped the last of *my* control.

My hips bucked, my fingers clenched in his hair, my moan was loud enough to hurt my ears.

Then he switched sides.

And my pleasure ramped, my pussy went liquid, the flames of desire made every muscle in my body clench.

I bucked again, knocking him back enough to reach for the nightstand and extract a condom from the box I kept there. I continued moving, pushing him to his back, yanking at the button and unzipping his jeans, working the material down enough to free his cock.

Tempting as a lollipop. I forced myself to focus on the next ten minutes rather than ten seconds.

One move had the condom wrapper torn open. The next, the latex ring pulled from the plastic square. One more to roll it down the pulsing thickness of his cock. My pussy clenched with need, my hands were still shaking, my brain was in a fog of desire, but when Pierce murmured, "Artie," I still froze and glanced up at him.

"You sure?" he asked softly.

In answer, I straddled his hips and guided him inside me.

Hard. Full. Deep.

We groaned as I bottomed out, and I paused, heart pounding, breaths coming in rapid inhalations and exhalations.

"Pierce?"

He grunted, eyes half-mast and hands coming up to cup my breasts.

"I'm"—his thumb dragged across my nipple and I groaned—"sure."

A grin that soaked into my skin, slid into the tiny crack he'd made in my hardened heart. "Then move, baby." One palm dropped to my hip, guiding me into motion.

I moved.

I forgot about the past. I forgot about my fear. I forgot about everything except the way it felt to be with Pierce, to have him inside me, to have his hands running up and down my body, to have his whispered words of encouragement in my ear, to feel how perfectly matched our bodies were.

I moved and he stroked, stoking the fires of my desire. I

moved and he gentled, slowing me, and by doing so driving that pleasure higher, making it more intense. I moved and he guided me effortlessly up and over the edge into orgasm.

I moved—

And suddenly was on my back, him pounding into me, my legs wrapping around him, my hands doing the stroking and coaxing and gentling, until finally he exploded inside me.

A groan. One, two, three more strokes.

His head dropped to my shoulder, hips stilling, hot breaths puffing on my skin.

Then another groan as he shifted to the side and cradled me against his chest.

Terrified.

I should be absolutely terrified.

Instead, my eyes slid closed and I fell headlong into oblivion.

And if I fell headlong into something else, something deeper, some heavy emotion that was winding its way tightly into my heart along with that sleep, then I wasn't ready to admit it yet.

LIDS FLYING OPEN, I sat up on a gasp.

Pierce was still in bed with me, though at some point he'd ditched his jeans and the condom, and had come back to pull the covers over us.

At my gasp, he instantly straightened by my side. "What's the matter?"

"Thomas!" I said, eyes darting around the room and fingers reaching for the blankets. "Kate!" We'd left them on the back deck while we—

Oh my God.

I was so going to hell.

Pierce chuckled, reaching for my hand and tugging me back to his chest.

I smacked him. "We can't do this," I said, frantic now. "They're out there and—"

"They went to Disneyland," he said.

My lips parted, but no words came out.

"Left about ten seconds after we started arguing." He held up his cell. "The plan was to convince you to come with us, but Kate called an audible and decided that leaving me here with no ride was the better move."

"Plan?" I asked, trying to process all of what he'd just said, but getting lost in the references to audibles and the happiest place on earth.

"My family decided they needed to play matchmaker."

Brows drawing together, I asked, "Um. What?"

Not the most articulate sentiment, but give a girl some credit here. I'd just woken up after some of the best sex of my life, and now I was inundated with sexy, naked Pierce smiling up at me, talking about Disneyland and football plays and matchmaking.

"Maybe matchmaking isn't so much the right word, as they decided it was time I got my head out of my ass and went after what I was longing for all these years."

I froze. "Pierce—"

He tapped me on the nose. "And cue panic."

"Well, yeah," I said, trying again to slip out of bed, but halted once again when his arm wound around my waist and tugged me back against his chest. "Your family? I mean— I—"

"They like you, sweetheart," he said and gently turned me in his arms. "They like *me* with you."

"All of the reasons we shouldn't pursue this still exist. My background—" I struggled for the words. "I don't know if I'll ever be able to have a real relationship with a man, Pierce. Even if that man is you."

"I'm not looking for guarantees."

I smacked my palm against the mattress. "Well, then what are you looking for? A fuck buddy? A person to curate your next project? A convenient lay when we're both in town?" I shook my head. "I'm not a traditional, put-a-ring-on-it, can't-wait-to-wear-that-white dress kind of girl. I have a life. I'm happy with that life."

Or at least I was until he'd strolled into that restaurant six years before.

Because the niggling in the back of my mind had begun then—the thought that perhaps, I could have something more than temporary.

He bracketed my wrists and tugged me back to face him. "You're not a fuck buddy, you're not a source for jobs." His breath was short and pissed off. "I like you, Artie. More than I've ever liked another woman. You're funny and thoughtful, smart as hell. Talented beyond belief. Is it so insane to think that someone might want to be in your life permanently for those reasons alone?"

"Yes!" I screamed.

Screamed.

Later, when I looked back at the moment, I wasn't proud of myself or the way I acted, but I was definitely proud of Pierce.

Because he just cupped my cheek, brushed my tangled mass of hair out of my eyes, and said, "Then I'll just have to show you."

FOURTEEN

Pierce

TWO DAYS.

Forty-eight hours and my life had taken a hard right.

Life was really weird sometimes.

Two days ago I'd been at the airport, excited to see my family and too scared to put myself out there for Artie. Today I was at my house, my nose filled with the glorious scents of my mom's special Christmas dinner—turkey, mashed potatoes, stuffing, deviled eggs, pea salad, and a collection of pies—and Artie was wrestling in the backyard with my nieces and nephews.

The night before, her eyes had filled with tears when I'd promised to show her that I could like her for who she was inside and not because of her past. I'd held her close, treated her gently, but I'd also deliberately changed the mood to lighter topics.

We'd had our fill of heavy for that day.

Light was what was needed.

So, I'd ordered some food on DoorDash, had cued up

Netflix on her TV, and we'd watched flat-earther documentaries and action movies until we'd both crashed.

This morning, I'd needed to get back to my family and surprisingly, Artie had agreed to come with me, rather than sending me home in a Lyft as I had expected. Though, that probably had to do with the picture of the chocolate pie my mom had texted. When I'd shown Artie, her eyes had lit up.

"It's better than her meatloaf," I'd cajoled.

She'd caved.

"Progress," my mom murmured, glancing out the window over the sink where I'd paused to watch Artie play with the kids.

I nodded. "Still a long way to go."

"Mmm." She whisked the gravy.

I knew that *mmm* and it didn't bode for good things. "What, Mom?"

More whisking, slightly faster. "Nothing."

"*Mom.*"

She sighed, tapped the whisk on the side of the saucepan before setting it aside. Then she turned to me. "Be sure, Pierce," she said. "Before you crack open that heart, make sure you're ready to catch it with both hands. This can't be a game or a case of wanting something you couldn't have. This has to be about her. And she deserves care."

Anger made the back of my throat tight. "You're the one who pushed me to make the first move."

My mom picked up the whisk again, began stirring. "I did."

"Well, you should know then that I care about her," I ground out. "I see who she is when she's forgotten to keep her guard up, and it's fucking wonderful. I want that in my life."

"And what about what she wants?"

What the fuck?

I blew out a sharp breath. "I don't know what she wants. I don't know if *she* knows what she wants. But I do know what she deserves. And that's a person to have her back and to care for her."

"Are you sure you can be that person?"

"Fuck, yes, I am."

I was spinning, life handing me another one of those curveballs. My mom had been all for me sweeping over to Artie's house the previous day, all for getting her to take a chance on me. Why now did it seem like my mom wanted me to step back?

"Are you sure?"

I clenched my hands into fists. "Yes."

"Okay."

My mom set the whisk down again and turned to face me, wrapping her arms around my neck and hugging me tight. "I'm happy for you, honey," she murmured. "I hope it works out." She pulled back, returned to the gravy, but at what was no doubt a bewildered expression on my face, her eyes softened. "She doesn't have anyone," my mom said by way of explanation. "She needed someone to look out for her. To make sure she's in good hands."

The frustration and anger faded from my body as understanding took root.

I wrapped my arms around her from behind, hugging her lightly as she stirred the gravy. It was a time-consuming recipe, but in cooking and in life, she never took shortcuts.

Never gave us less than what we needed.

I'd never wondered if she loved us.

And now she was extending that same care to Artie. Fuck, but I was lucky to have her in my life.

"I love you, Mom."

She patted my arm.

"Love you, too." Then she nudged me back. "Now, get that table set."

Grinning, I dropped my arms and headed to the cabinets.

———————

ARTIE HAD STAYED through dinner but had cried off during the present opening.

I didn't protest her leaving or try and convince her to stay—

The nieces and nephews had done more than enough of that on their own. I did, however, take notice of the fatigue etching into the corners of her eyes and took pity on Artie, helping her gather her things and walking her out.

"I'm leaving in the morning," she murmured, pausing just outside the front door. "Iceland for the reshoots and then I'll be in New York for a few days to make sure the filming of *Pop* is progressing."

I tugged a strand of hair out of her face. "How many projects do you have right now?"

"Five," she said with a guilty look. "But *Frost* is almost done," she added, naming the film she was heading to Iceland for. "*Pop* is under control, and *Carrot* is in your capable hands."

I lifted a brow. "And the other two?"

She glared. "Why am I suddenly feeling guilty?"

"You shouldn't." I kissed her forehead, meaning it. I didn't want her to *not* work. It was critically important, and she should do what she wanted. However, I also didn't want her to burn out. "I just know you have a lot on your plate."

She wrinkled her nose and it was cute enough that I kissed it.

"You're annoying," she said, swatting me away.

"You're beautiful."

A sigh. "Charming."

I grinned. "That's a good thing."

"My other two projects are in development. I won't have anything major until probably the summer." She narrowed her eyes in my direction before walking down the steps and heading toward her car. "Someone's schedule necessitated shooting a certain film in Scotland before the end of the year, and so I had to double-dip."

I caught her hand, tugged her back to my chest. "I can think of something I want to *double-dip*."

"Ew." She stopped struggling for a moment and glanced up at me again, nose in the cute wrinkle for the second time in as many minutes.

I considered her reaction alongside my words. Then nodded. "I think that *ew* is warranted."

She laughed, shook her head, and kept walking. "You're a piece of work, Pierce Daniels."

"That I am."

Another laugh. "That wasn't a compliment."

"Still took it as one."

Her driver's door automatically unlocked, and she tugged it open, snagging her purse and jacket from my arms and tossing them onto the passenger's seat. "Unbelievable." She whipped around, finger pressing to my lips before I could say that was a compliment.

I nipped at her finger.

She shivered, eyes going hot.

"I know we agreed to go slow—"

A snort. "Is that what the kids are calling last night these days?"

My lips curved. "Definitely," I murmured and leaned down. "So, slow or not, I'm going to kiss you now, and because I'm not going to see you for a week, I'm going to make it count."

Her hands rested on my chest, she drifted a little closer. "Pierce—"

I let my mouth swallow the rest of her words.

My tongue slid across her bottom lip, dipped inside her mouth. Her hands lifted and slid into my hair, her lips moving against mine, her body shifting until it was pressed to mine from hips to chest. And I kissed her, long and hot and demanding. I put everything I was feeling into that kiss. How much I liked her, how much I wanted her, how much I *needed* her.

And she gave back.

Her tongue met mine stroke for stroke, her hands gripped tight.

Eventually, however, we had to breathe and so I released her mouth, allowing us the opportunity to inhale some much-needed oxygen.

Artie released a shuddering breath, pressed the back of her hand to her reddened cheeks. "I think I like how the kids do slow."

Considering that we'd somehow ended up with our positions reversed, my shoulders pressed against the frame of the car with Artie in front of me, one foot on the floorboard, the other leg wrapped around my thigh as we'd kissed, I could concur.

Regrettably, she stepped down. "Why do I always end up climbing you like a tree when we kiss?"

I pushed away from the car, cupped her cheek. "Not hating it, sweetheart."

Her reddened cheeks went redder. "I blame you. You're younger and thus, more dangerous."

"I'll take the distinction if it means you'll keep kissing me like that."

She smiled and wrapped her arms around my middle, squeezing me for a long moment. Then she stepped back and lowered herself into the driver's seat. "I'll see you in Scotland."

I nodded. "I'll call you before then."

Surprise registered across her features. "But I'll see you—"

Reaching across her, I buckled her seat belt then stopped on my lean back to press another quick kiss to her lips. "Perk number 652 about being in a relationship?"

Her brows drew down. "Unnecessary phone calls?"

"Necessary calls to get to know each other and stay apprised of what's happening in each other's lives." I grinned at her put-upon expression. "Along with texts."

"I might not always pick up," she grumbled.

Apparently, she hated talking on the phone. See? Something new I'd learned about her.

I shrugged. "So call or text when you can."

Her face relaxed, and I stole one last kiss before straightening. "Okay."

"Want to know perk number 653?" I asked, pausing as I'd started to swing the door closed.

Artie shook her head and sighed, but her mouth was twitching. "Sure."

"Perk number 653 is that we can have sexy FaceTime time."

I waggled my brows.

Her laughter trailed me as I shut the door, wrapped firmly around my heart as I walked back into the house, stayed close as I navigated the remaining days until I could see her again.

FIFTEEN

Pierce: How's Iceland? Icy?

Four hours later.

Pierce: I think you're testing my resolve. Text me when you can.

The next morning.

Artie: Iceland is icy (I'm taking your pun and running with it)
Pierce: How are the reshoots?
Artie: Disaster. The crew's equipment got stolen.
Pierce: WTF
Artie: Also, the intern who left the trailer unlocked as easy pickings was let go.
Pierce: Seems reasonable.
Artie: Considering this is the second time it happened, then yes.
Pierce: Was it insured?
Artie: Thankfully, yes. And we hadn't begun shooting yet, so nothing on that front was lost. Though, I hope when you're

trolling eBay for new camera equipment, you'll recognize ours and buy it.

Pierce: Next time I buy my stuff off eBay, I'll be sure to let you know.

Artie: *laughing emoji* Thanks.

Pierce: I'm guessing you haven't been to bed yet.

Artie: Nope. Not yet. I basically landed and was pulled into the case of the missing equipment.

Pierce: Well, then I should let you go and get some rest. I'll text you tomorrow.

Artie: Pierce?

Pierce: Yeah?

Artie: *photo*

Pierce:

Artie: Did you not get it?

Pierce:

Artie: Pierce?

Pierce: I'm . . . holy shit, sweetheart. I think you just made my century with that.

Artie: *blushing emoji*

Pierce: Am I going to get to see that outfit in person?

Artie: You mean me naked? Yes, I think that can be arranged.

Pierce: Thank you, sweet baby Jesus.

Artie: Good night—or day, anyway.

The next day

Artie: I hope that your phone is on Do Not Disturb. But I just wanted to tell you that the equipment was found!

Pierce: That's awesome!

Artie: Oh shit, I woke you up, didn't I?

Pierce: No. I was up. With my family being here, work has been nonexistent. I stayed up late and was trying to catch up.

Artie: Isn't this supposed to be your week off?

Pierce: Technically.

Artie: And who's the workaholic now?

Pierce: There isn't any rest for the weary, at least when it comes to emails. But I'm actually just finishing up.

Artie: Well, then I'm going to let you go to sleep.

Pierce: You doing okay, sweetheart?

Artie: I'm a lot better than yesterday.

Pierce: Good.

Artie: Good night, Pierce.

A minute later

Artie: Oh, you still up?

Pierce: Yes, sweetheart.

Artie: I know I kind of suck at this dating thing. Texting in the middle of the night, taking a full day to reply back to you. But . . . it's kind of nice knowing that you're at the other end of the line.

Pierce: And that right there.

Artie: ? And what right there?

Pierce: You may think you don't know how to be in a relationship, but your words tell me differently.

Artie: Oh.

Pierce: Yeah. *Oh.*

Artie:

Pierce: Goodnight, sweetheart.

Artie: Goodnight.

SIXTEEN

Pierce

MY PHONE RANG APPROXIMATELY two seconds after I got off the plane.

I shifted my rolling bag to my other hand, fished my cell out of my pocket, saw it was Artie, and quickly swiped my finger across the screen.

"Hey, sweetheart," I said, putting it up to my ear.

"Oh," she said. "I didn't think you'd pick up."

I grinned. "Should I hang up and let you call again so you can leave a message?"

"Uh . . ." She faltered. "I— um—"

"I'm kidding."

"Oh."

I'd called her the night before on my way to the airport, but unsurprisingly she hadn't picked up, considering it was the middle of the night in Iceland.

"You heading to New York?"

"My flight's in the morning."

"Reshoots going a little smoother then?"

Her voice relaxed. "Yes," she said. "I'm guessing they'll have them wrapped up in a week or ten days at most."

"That's good news."

"Yeah."

Someone pushed past me. "Were you calling for a reason, honey? I'm loving hearing your voice, but I just got off the plane."

"Oh, I'm sorry. It's not important. This is an inconvenient time. I'll just—"

"Artie."

"—let you go. I shouldn't have—"

"*Artie.*"

She stopped.

"If we waited for a convenient time for both of us, I don't think we'd ever talk again."

A beat. "True."

"So, sweetheart, what's up?"

"I, um, was just returning your call."

"Well, I was just calling because I wanted to hear your voice," I said, walking forward, my lips curved into a giant smile. "That, and my family liked having you at my house."

"Your family *is* pretty great," she said, relaxing into the conversation. "A certain youngest son aside."

"Rude."

I went down the escalator, approaching customs and passport control and knowing that I'd need to end the call, even though I didn't want to.

"Now I'm not going to have my mom overnight you that chocolate pie."

She gasped. "You're a monster."

"And I'm still not hearing any sweet nothings," I teased.

"You're the best Daniels, aside from your fabulous baking mother, and the mostest talented director I've ever met, and—"

She broke off and I almost heard the blush over the airwaves, even before I heard her next words.

"What's that?" I coaxed.

"And you also give the best oral of any man I've ever allowed the pleasure of licking my pussy."

My jaw dropped open.

I know it did.

Also, my cock twitched.

"If you get your ass to Scotland, I'll do it again."

"Promise?"

"You promise to *allow* me?" I asked, lips twitching.

She snorted. "Not exactly a trial."

"Well, then. Yes. I promise." A beat. "Also, I think there might be a chocolate pie in your future."

"My hero."

I chuckled. "Okay, well, unfortunately this hero has to go get my passport checked out. I'll call you later, all right?"

"All right."

"I wish you were here already." I went for sweet.

She tossed sass back in my direction, and I loved it. "You just want to get your tongue inside me."

Another chuckle. Another cock twitch.

"Bye, baby," she murmured.

Another pulse in my heart.

Why did I wish those three things were my future?

All I knew was if they were, without a doubt, they would be the best part.

SEVENTEEN

Artie

NEW YORK WAS EASY.

And since the time change was easier to manage, Pierce and I spoke every day. Usually for just a couple of minutes, but there was one night where both of our schedules aligned, and we talked for almost two hours.

Me. On the phone.

With a man.

Not talking about work.

Or, well, not talking about work all that *much*.

But we'd discussed *Carrot*, of course, and *Pop*, and his prep for filming the sequel to the superhero flick he'd wrapped the previous year—the reason shooting for *Carrot* was happening when it was.

But then we'd talked about his family, about how his parents and sisters had been filled with equal parts outrage and gratitude when he'd presented them with a vacation for the following summer. We'd joked about the silly stuff in our daily lives—the craft service table not having the right kind of cheese according to my lead on *Pop*, Pierce's childhood friend trying to convince him that he had the best script ever written in the history of all scripts (and one that had very nearly approached a porno, both for the sheer quantity of sex scenes and also the minimal amounts of dialogue).

We'd talked about our moms.

How lucky we both felt to have them, even though they each had their faults.

Dorinne was often exacting, and though that came from a place of obvious love, the pressure she'd placed on her kids to be successful had been a lot.

Not that the kids had ended up worse for wear, with Pierce being who he was and Kate and Marie both lovely and successful in their own roles as a mother and a lawyer.

But the standards had been high.

My story was different obviously.

My mom's love wasn't quite as . . . altruistic? Maybe that wasn't fair because it was there, even though it was unhealthy. I'd had to be more parent than child, a partner in our survival.

That was more than any child should shoulder.

And that was putting aside the fact that she'd stayed with an abuser.

I'd learned to separate the two over the years, understood my mother wasn't healthy, wasn't strong or resourceful or gritty.

I could be angry she exposed me to that, angry she stayed and dismantled my life in order to stay with an abuser. And I *was* angry. I was furious she hadn't prioritized someone she was supposed to have loved unconditionally over sick wants and needs.

Kids were innocent.

I'd been innocent.

And my parents had torn that away.

But as an adult, I had more clarity. My mom had been troubled, and though she'd loved me in her own way, her actions had often been inexcusable. But I either had to hold on to the good and compartmentalize the bad away, or I risked being overwhelmed by my anger.

So, I chose to remember the way she'd saved up to buy the ingredients to make my favorite ice cream cake for my birthday. How she'd braided my hair before bed every night so it wouldn't get tangled. The way she'd let me cuddle with her in her bed when I'd had a nightmare and was scared.

Small things.

But important when taken into account with the rest.

And because of that, I also understood that the hole she'd left behind when she'd taken her own life would never fully be filled.

It was inevitable.

It was sad.

It was just the way things were.

"Please, ensure that your seatbacks are in the upright and locked position . . ."

I blinked, pulling myself out of my memories. I'd gone years without thinking about my parents, deliberately shoving all thoughts of them down and locking them up with chains and steel cables.

Pierce had changed that.

He'd peeled back the armor, exposed my vulnerable underbelly, but instead of feeling flayed open, now I was . . . lighter?

Pierce knew everything.

And he still kept calling and texting.

I smiled and stowed my laptop, zipping it into my bag and stowing it safely under the seat in front of mine. The plane was descending rapidly, and my pulse was thundering, the thought of seeing Pierce after nearly two weeks was both exhilarating and terrifying.

"Nervous flyer?"

I glanced at the older woman sitting next to me in first class —don't judge, I flew a lot and that meant I was going to be comfortable, high cost or not—and smiled. "Oh, no," I said. "I'm not nervous about flying. I travel all the time."

"It's a man."

I blinked at her in surprise. "I'm sorry, what?"

She laughed. "I've only ever seen that expression for two things—flying and the opposite sex."

"I—" I shook my head. "It's not really that. I mean, I'm fine."

She lifted one white brow until it almost touched the edge of her curly, permed hair. "Of course, you're fine," she said. "Doesn't mean there isn't a man in your life who's got you on tenterhooks." A smile that made creases appear at the corners of her eyes. "I'm Beverly."

"Artemis." I stuck out my hand. "Nice to meet you."

"You too, dear," Beverly said.

"So, what's bringing you to Scotland?"

Another warm smile. "Vacation." A beat. "And a man."

I grinned.

"What about you?"

"Work." I paused then figured, what the hell. "And a man."

Beverly laughed and clapped her hands. "I love it when I'm right. Okay, okay, tell me everything. How'd you meet him? What does he look like? Is he loaded?"

"He does okay," I said. "But I think I probably have been around longer." I grinned at her perplexed look. "I produce films for a living."

Her eyes widened. "Anything I've seen?"

I named a few of my more popular films.

Those eyes went wider. "Wow. I've never met a real-life movie star before."

I grinned. "Definitely not a star. I just present the stories to the actors and directors. They're the ones who bring them to life."

"It's still amazing," Beverly gushed. "How did you get into it?"

The truth burned a hole in the back of my mind, but I forced my lips to curve up into a smile. "I got lucky." A beat. "And worked hard."

Beverly patted my arm. "I bet you did," she murmured, and I frowned briefly at the tone, but then she began talking again, quicker and more enthusiastically. "Okay, that was work, so now I want to know the really juicy bits. Who's the man?"

I shook my head. "It's silly and really new. I'm—" I sighed. "Truthfully, I'm not even sure what we are. Dating? Boyfriend-girlfriend?" *Lovers? More?* I thought, though didn't say that aloud. "I just know that I've never really been interested in more than temporaries with a man . . . until Pierce."

Lips curved up. "Based on the blush on your face, I'm guessing he's attractive?"

"The most gorgeous man I've seen in my lifetime," I said.

"Is he an actor?" Beverly asked. "They tend to be . . ."

"On the pretty end of the spectrum?" I said with a smile, to which she nodded. "Not an actor. A director and brilliantly talented."

"Should I repeat my previous question and ask if he's made anything I might have seen?"

I laughed. "Sure. And yes, if you've seen or heard of—" I named Pierce's huge box office superhero film.

"Really?"

I nodded. "Really."

"Wow," she said. "A power couple in the making."

"I don't know about that," I replied as the plane hit the runway with a bump, both of us fighting the lean forward as we came to a halting stop. The next few minutes were spent taxiing to the gate then gathering our things—another perk of first-class flying meant we got off the plane quickly.

"Well, it was nice to meet you," I said as we went our separate ways.

"You too, Artemis," Beverly said, smiling widely up at me. "Meeting you just absolutely made my week."

It wouldn't be until later that I found out why exactly I'd made Beverly's week.

And it broke my heart.

EIGHTEEN

Pierce

IT WAS AN ENTIRELY different animal working with Artie on set.

I felt her presence the whole day.

Not in a frustrating or oppressive way, but my body was very much in tune with the fact that she was there, and she was close, and . . . I couldn't touch her yet.

She'd arrived on set that evening, when we'd still had several hours left to shoot, and had been totally professional. Friendly, curious about how things were going, but also distant.

Which hadn't been a surprise, exactly.

Our relationship wasn't public and on set, the film had to come first.

Hadn't meant I wasn't aching to tug her into a private corner and kiss her until she lost all control and tried to climb me like a tree again.

Instead, I was forced to content myself with a kiss on her cheek and a quick hug before we got back to work. The shot list that evening was going to be a tough one, balancing the need for enough light to show what Eden was doing—in this case ferreting secret messages to the Allied forces during World War II along a rugged coastline that was supposed to replicate France, because we didn't have the budget to shoot in both France and Scotland. She'd have several scenes hiding from pursuers, a few more in frantically preparing messages, and an emotional one where she had to leave behind a friend who'd helped her.

Later in the week there would be a water scene, my heroine being picked up by Nazi forces, just after she safely sends a message with their next Allied targets enclosed, and the viewer would be left wondering what happened to our hero as the Allied troops scrambled to get into position to meet their foes.

Spoiler alert—she'd be rescued by the friend she'd been forced to leave behind, and both would return safely back to Scotland.

But those scenes would be filmed in two weeks.

Tonight was fleeing and hiding and transcribing by torchlight.

The only thing I was looking less forward to was the boat scene.

Still, we managed to get through them with minimal takes and Rhonda, Artie's suggestion for director of cinematography, did a fabulous job of capturing the wonderful acting Eden was giving. The scenes were beautiful, the tension palpable, the leaving of her friend heartbreaking.

I was immensely proud of our team, but we were all exhausted and ready for the day tomorrow . . . or well, for the rest of *that* day.

The next call time would be a full twenty-six hours from now, and I fully intended to spend them in Artie's hotel room.

Wrapping up only took me another fifteen minutes, and I looked around for Artie as I headed for my car, feeling disappointment sweep over me when I didn't spot her anywhere. We hadn't made plans to meet up, and it was late, after she'd had a full day of travel. She'd probably gone back to the hotel and was catching up on much-needed sleep.

Which I'd been hoping to do.

With her.

Sighing, I tugged open the driver's door and collapsed into the seat. One movement to turn on the ignition, the next to buckle in.

"Hey."

I jumped.

Nothing to explain it away. I startled and whirled in the seat, spinning to see Artie sitting next to me, legs primly crossed, hands folded neatly on top of a set of files in her lap.

But her smile was anything but prim.

"You ready to put those superior oral skills to the test?" Her teeth nibbled at the corner of her mouth. "Or maybe you're too tired."

I grinned. "I don't think I'll ever be too tired for that."

"Good." Her eyes darted from side to side when I just continued to stare at her. "Um. Are we going to go?"

My hand came up, cupping her cheek and running my thumb across the silky skin of her jaw. "You're beautiful."

Her eyes dropped.

"Missed you."

Pretty blue eyes back on mine. "We're new."

For once, I wasn't on that same wavelength. "What do you mean, sweetheart?"

"I—um—well, don't you think it's a little early to be really missing me? I mean, we haven't really even been on a date yet."

"You've met my family," I countered.

"Still not a date."

I slid my hand down her throat, her arm, linking our fingers together and squeezing lightly. "Well, in that case, I guess I owe you a date."

Her head shook. "That's not what I meant," she said quickly. "I—"

"I know." A beat. "But we've been working toward this for more than half a decade, I think that means we can agree to miss each other when we're not together."

She traced her thumb over the back of my hand. "I do like talking to you on the phone."

"How many dates does that put us at if we consider more than five years of me pining and all the text and phone calls over the last few weeks?"

"Three," she said.

"Three?" I repeated, eyes wide.

Her smile was sultry. "Yup. Three," she affirmed. "Because I heard that's the magic number for women to put out." Chagrin crept into the edges of that grin. "Well, women who don't put out on the first date, that is."

"I seem to remember you saying that age is just a number at some point." I squeezed her hand lightly and reached for the gear shift. "Shouldn't that number attitude also apply to dating?"

She considered that as I pulled away from the set and onto the road. "I'll concede the point."

"Victory is mine!" I said, adding my best evil laughter for effect.

"Oh lord," she muttered. "A younger man. What have I gotten myself into?"

"Superior oral skills and boundless energy?"

Her lips curved. "Oh, yeah. That." A blip of quiet. "How soon until we'll be back at the hotel?"

I pressed the accelerator down just a bit more firmly.

THE NEXT FEW days passed in a blur of filming and fucking.

Ha.

My two favorite things.

But by the weekend, the entire crew had one final day off before the last push to finish up the movie. I was thrilled with how the dailies were looking, and it was beyond amazing working with Artie on a project like this. She was an excellent producer. I'd known that, of course, solely from reputation and how we'd worked together during the lead up to filming, but it was a different animal altogether when it came down to being with someone day in and day out, navigating stressful circumstances.

Artie seemed to take it all in stride.

When our lead, Eden, had a breakdown, she took her off to the side so they could talk it out.

When the local police came out, unhappy that the crew's equipment was in a field—even though it had been permitted and preapproved by the council—she handled it with aplomb, charming the officers with craft services, and giving the chief constable a cameo in the film.

When it rained for two days straight, we sat together and reworked the schedule so we could get what we needed in the minimum amount of time in the elements.

It was easy.

She wasn't one of those producers that took over or micromanaged or threw hissy fits because she didn't agree with someone else's vision. She trusted the people she'd put in place, and she complimented the process as a whole.

But tonight was our final day off before we headed down the home stretch, and I was going to make it count.

With a date.

I grinned and towel-dried my hair, having slipped back to my room for a quick shower and to change while Artie had been on a conference call.

I knew she'd been teasing about me owing her a date, but it was true that our courtship had been anything but . . . courtship. We'd fallen into bed, had limited contact, then had slowly built a friendship. Then my family had cornered her in the airport, and we'd jumped into . . . something intense. So, no, we hadn't had a first date, but this was an oversight I intended to remedy.

First with flowers. Then with a gift—and not jewelry because while my girl did have a certain appreciation for all things sparkly and gem-related, based on what I'd seen her wearing at awards shows and industry events over the years, I also knew that wasn't the way to her heart.

I picked up the bouquet of flowers and the envelope with the script I'd scored the rights to, shoved my cell and wallet into my pockets, then headed back out of my room, feeling lighter than I had in years.

First, I was working on a project I was really excited about.

Second, I was working on that with Artemis.

Third, we were going on a date that would hopefully make her smile.

Tucking the envelope under my arm, I knocked softly at her door. She answered, eyes warm, phone still on speaker in the background. I handed her the flowers and she took them, blowing me a kiss. Hesitating on the threshold, I mime-asked if I should leave, but she shook her hand and waved me in, holding up two fingers and mouthing, "Two more minutes."

Moving to the bed, I sat on its edge, trying to get my mind off the fact that I'd put my so-called oral skills to work on it just that morning. This was not about that. It was about giving Artie what she deserved.

And also, not to be all woo-woo-my-feelings-are-*so*-important, but it was also about allowing myself to have what *I* deserved and wanted.

Six years ago, I'd felt like I'd had the greatest treasure in the world only to have it torn away. Now I was getting a chance to build something with the woman I'd been in love with practically since the moment she'd given me the first shovelful of sass and *definitely* since she'd given me the book whose adaptation we were currently filming.

We both needed slow.

Me to trust that she wouldn't retreat again.

Her to trust that she didn't need to.

And for that, we got a date—or well, hopefully the first of many dates when our schedules allowed for them. But for tonight, it was about us and eating good food and laughing and talking and—

"Awfully serious after such a good day," came a husky voice in my ear.

I shivered, turned to press a kiss to her jaw. "You call being stuck outside in the driving rain a good day?"

"When we capture what we did," she said, weaving her hands into my hair, "then yes."

Shifting my head slightly, she kissed me and just like every other time our mouths touched, all the thoughts disappeared from my mind. I could only focus on her floral scent surrounding me, her soft lips against mine, the slight sting from her fingernails against my scalp.

She pressed me down onto the mattress.

And I wasn't going to lie, it wasn't like I was trying very hard to stop her.

A hot handful of Artie on top of me? Yeah, I'd take that every time.

Her palms slid down to my chest, worked at the buttons of the shirt I'd put on, all while her pelvis moved against mine and her tongue was deep in my mouth. I reached down to grip her hips then winced when the back of my hand was jabbed by something sharp.

The envelope.

The date.

A very sexy and turned-on Artie.

We could—

I mentally smacked myself on the back of my head in a move that was very similar to what my mom would have done if she'd been there and slowed the kiss, pushing us both back up to sitting.

"What?" she said, pulling back slightly.

"As much as I like kissing you," I said. "I wanted to give you something."

"Besides the flowers?" she asked.

I nodded, extracted the slightly crumpled, but still mostly intact envelope out from under my hips, and handed it to her.

Brows pulling together, she took it, her eyes searching mine as she opened the flap and extracted the script.

Nerves suddenly hit, and hard. I remembered that she couldn't stand a lot of my films, even though I adored and had learned so many things from the projects she'd done, from the way she managed to make films that always captured elements of the characters that made them distinctly human and yet distinctively captivating.

I thought she might like this one.

But what if it was shit?

She'd given me *Carrot*, and I'd give her . . . manure.

I resisted the urge to snag it from her hands. "You probably won't like it," I said. "I just thought . . . anyway, you don't have to—"

Her finger dropped to my lips. "Shh."

"The physical stuff is easy," she murmured, stroking her

hand lightly over the top sheet of the script. "It's all the rest of it, that's scary."

I sucked in a breath.

She rested her hand on my thigh. "I know you've been the one to make a lot of the big leaps, dragging me along next to you in tiny baby steps, but I'm in this, Pierce. I'm not saying I'm not scared my past will affect us or that I'll panic and ruin things. I'm not sure I can live my life in something that isn't temporary. But I also know that I never even understood that I might be missing out on something by living in temporaries until I met you."

"Sweetheart."

She shushed me again. "I might as well get this all out. I knew the moment you strolled into that meeting six years ago that you were different. I knew that you could burrow in, could be dangerous, and yet I still took your hand and brought you back to my apartment." Her lips twitched. "I ran afterward, of course. Because I'm good at running, good at avoiding everything by just keeping my head down and working and working and *working*. But you were always there, Pierce. I fought so hard to make it just friends between us because I knew that you had the potential for more, and I was"—a sharp breath—"*still am* terrified."

"I'd be lying if I didn't say I wasn't terrified right along with you," I told her, wrapping my arms around her and tugging her close. I bit back the words, the fact that I wanted to tell her that I loved her so fucking much. This wasn't the time to press further. This was my chance to bolster her, to support the fact that she'd put it all out there and had made herself vulnerable.

"Words of comfort," she quipped, nuzzling my throat.

"Words of truth," I said. "And that's how we'll move forward. Slow and easy and with honesty. If something's not working, we talk about it."

"And what do we do when our schedules make it so we can't?" she asked. "I've seen couples who have a hell of a lot fewer problems than we have not make it because they're apart too much."

There was a lot to unpack in that statement.

"First," I said. "What are all these problems that we're having?"

She leaned back, began ticking off on fingers. "Our ages, for one. Our backgrounds, for another. The fact that we work in such an insane place as Hollywood. Temptations on film sets. Pressure and budgets and—"

"So, work is your major concern." I didn't touch the age thing yet.

A sigh then, "Yes, I guess it is."

"Have you ever had an on-set romance?" I asked and when she shook her head, I chuckled. "Me neither. Because I tend to leave those to the actors."

"That's not to say—"

"That's not to say *a lot of things*. People cheat or they don't, and I think there are circumstances in many careers that can make it easier or harder."

"That's true."

"The difference with us is that I hope we can make a pact to be honest with each other if this isn't working." Not that I thought it wouldn't work or that I would let her go if it wasn't— because, yeah no—but I also knew Artie needed the out. She needed to have an escape plan.

I could give that to her.

Even if I never intended to let her use it.

She nodded. "We've always been good at talking things out."

"Yeah, babe," I murmured and pressed a kiss to her forehead. "We have. Now, about our schedules. We're both used to this life, we both know the deal. I can't think of someone who would be a better fit to be in my life. The last person I dated couldn't cope with the time away, and I'm not saying I enjoy not being with you, but I also know you get it." I tugged at a strand of her hair. "And I would never do anything to undermine your career because I understand it. So, if we need more time together, we arrange our schedules to make that happen. If we can't, we FaceTime or text or call when we can."

"You make it sound easy."

I grinned. "I'm good at faking it until I make it."

She rolled her eyes. "The most comforting words a woman can hear from a potential boyfriend."

"You asked and you shall receive," I said, tugging her to her feet and slipping the script from her hands, setting it on the nightstand. "Come on."

"Where are we going?"

"I owe you a first date," I told her. "And we're going to miss our dinner reservations unless we leave now."

She glanced down at herself. "What? I'm wearing jeans and a smelly T-shirt." Her fingers went to her hair. "And a messy bun—"

I kissed her. "Beautiful," I murmured. "And the place is casual."

"So, why are you wearing a nice shirt?" Her eyes narrowed in the direction of my button-down.

I did up the couple of buttons she'd opened. "Because it's more fun for you to take it off."

"Making me work for it?" A huff.

"You're the one who keeps bringing up the age difference," I teased. "I gotta make sure my girl stays healthy."

Her head tilted to the side. "Your idea of my exercising is to take your clothes off?"

"Yup."

That head shook, lips tilting up. "Okay," she said. "I think I'm on board with that."

"Good." I touched the tip of her nose.

"Good. Now give me thirty seconds to make myself presentable for this date." She coaxed me back then reached up and released her hair from the messy bun, shaking it so it fell in waves down her back. A second later, she'd slipped off her T-shirt and tossed it to the floor. I tried to keep my eyes on her face, but it would have been a lie if I'd said I didn't let my gaze travel south to all that black lace and didn't enjoy the view for several long moments. By then, she rummaged through her closet and extracted a silky indigo blouse. She tugged it over her head, fluffed her hair once more, and shoved her feet into flats.

That thirty-second change might have been the sexiest thing I'd ever seen.

Not just because I'd been given a glimpse into something that was private, but also because of the confident way she'd done it. Artie was comfortable with her body and it showed in her movements, her composure, and also the fact that getting ready didn't mean locking herself into the bathroom for an hour. Not that I would have really minded that, because that would have been her choice, but it was also nice that she didn't feel that need.

No extra barriers required.

Just her and me.

Yeah, that was pretty damned perfect.

NINETEEN

Artie

TO MY SURPRISE, we didn't get into Pierce's rental and drive into the city proper.

Instead, we walked a few blocks down the road and around the corner to a tiny pub where he held open the door and waved to the man behind the bar and called a familiar, "Hey, Liam."

"Pierce," the man said. "Right through to the back."

"Thanks, bud."

Liam lifted his chin and Pierce took my hand, leading me through the pub and into a small room in the back. It was filled with tables, but they were all empty with the exception of one, which had a tiny placard that said Reserved sitting atop it.

He pulled out my chair, settling me into it with a wink and an, "I'm doing this first date thing right," then took his own seat.

I opened my mouth to ask him the question that had been swirling in my mind since the hotel room, but I didn't get a chance because a girl swept into the room and the next few minutes were spent being handed menus and ordering drinks.

Then she left and we both spent some time looking at those

menus, deciding what to order. And just as I'd started to open my mouth again to ask the question, she was back with our drinks.

I stifled my sigh.

Patience, young Jedi.

Pierce waited until she set the glasses down to ask, "Would you be able to give us five minutes? My girlfriend is trying to tell me something."

My jaw fell open. "How did you—?"

Breaking off with a shake of my hand, I barely heard the girl's reply or felt her leave. My eyes were on Pierce.

He covered my hand with his. "I know you, sweetheart."

I sighed, a reluctant smile on my lips. "You do," I said. "Sometimes better than I know myself, I think."

"That's a good thing."

I lifted a brow. "Is it though?"

He just grinned in reply and so I figured I might as well get on with what I'd been trying to tell him. "I keep bringing up the age thing?"

His expression sobered.

My heart sank. "Shit, I do, don't I?" I made a disgusted noise. "Ugh, all this talk about age not mattering and me just being with a person and not giving a damn if I'm older or they are . . . and it's all bullshit."

His hand covering mine twitched. "It's not bullshit," he said. "But I think it's probably a good idea to think about where it comes from."

"Yeah," I muttered, "it comes from me being a total hypocrite."

"Does it though?"

I pulled my hand back, narrowed my eyes. "I thought self-reflection is for the actors. You and I are supposed to be more transactional in our relationships."

"And would it make you feel better if it *was* transactional?"

"Ugh!" I stood up, pacing away and then back. "No. Yes. Fuck." I dropped my chin to my chest. "This isn't about age at all," I said. "It's about me trying to erect as many barriers between us as possible."

"Is it?"

"Don't push it, Pierce."

He grinned, the stink.

"Yes," I grumbled. "It's about barriers and staying safe and . . . I don't like self-reflection."

"I think you're good at self-reflection," he said. "It's what gives you your eye for film. I also think that you've done what we've all done, and that's shut away the stuff that is too scary or painful to deal with." He took a sip of his beer while I pondered that. "The trouble with shutting it all away, I think, is that it is going to burst free at some point."

I pouted. "You're supposed to be younger and stupider."

He laughed. "Is that your cue telling me we've had enough heavy for tonight?"

"You tell me," I said. "You're the one who supposedly knows me so well."

"You're done."

I was.

Just not nearly done with Pierce. Not by a long shot.

———

AFTER A DELICIOUS AND CARB-FILLED—THE man really did know me—meal, Pierce and I strolled hand-in-hand out of the pub.

It was dark and cloudy, mist hanging in the air and foreshadowing more rain in the coming days. But it wouldn't be as tricky to deal with since our location filming was complete.

We'd move into the studio, lock everything down, and then move onto the next project.

For the first time ever, that thought made me sad.

Thus was the power of Pierce.

Because for the first time ever, I also felt hope.

Being a weeknight, the streets were quiet and so we were the only ones on our stretch of sidewalk when he tugged me to a stop.

"What—?"

My back was suddenly flat against the brick wall of a building, Pierce's body pressed into mine and his mouth slamming down. He kissed me like a man on fire, tongue darting beyond my lips, tangling with mine. His fingers of one hand gripped my jaw, angling my head so he could take my mouth at just the right angle, while the other slid down to my hip.

I didn't need any coaxing.

My typical response to Pierce's mouth reigned supreme as I lifted my legs and wrapped them tightly around his hips, climbing him like a tree and completely losing myself in the kiss, in his mouth and teeth and tongue.

It was heat. It was desire. It was me and him.

A light flashed behind my closed lids then another. I wasn't sure if it was my pent-up passion or if it was a car turning onto the street. Either way, it seemed to remind us both that we were in the middle of the street.

"Trouble," he murmured as he drew away, sliding his palm down one leg and helping me lower it then the other to the ground.

I smiled up at him. "That's *your* middle name. You started it."

"Maybe." He took my hand. "Let's get out of this drizzle."

"Good plan," I teased. "I have thoughts for how we can pass the time when we get back to my room."

"Reading that script?"

"Reading *something*." I shook my head. "Bad attempt at innuendo. I'll leave those to you."

He squeezed my fingers. "Good idea."

"How about we just go back to the hotel, you give me multiple orgasms, and then we stay up late and read that script that you brought me?"

Pierce grinned. "Sounds like the best night ever."

We walked back to the hotel.

He gave me three—three!—orgasms.

Then we stayed up into the wee hours of the night reading the script, fighting and brainstorming and talking over taking it on as our next project together.

Staying up late is why we didn't see the news story.

Why we didn't hear our cell phones.

Why chaos was allowed to descend while we quietly slept in each other's arms.

TWENTY

Pierce

MY FIRST INDICATION that something was wrong was the pounding on the door. I blinked groggily, shifting my arm carefully to extract it from where it was trapped beneath Artie's sleeping form.

Shaking out the pins and needles, I walked to the door in nothing more than my underwear, not checking the peephole in an effort to get whoever was banging to shut the hell up and not wake Artie.

That turned out to be my second mistake.

I flicked the dead bolt to the side, yanked the door open, and then blinked at shock at what was there.

At *who* was there.

Clicking.

It was the clicking that brought me out of my stupor, out of seeing a group of men in the hall outside the hotel room, black eyes of their cameras taking pictures of me in my underwear.

But I didn't react quickly enough because then I heard her.

"Pierce. What's—"

"No!" I whipped around, started to close the door.

Too late.

"Artemis. Look here! Artemis!"

She froze, sheet tucked around her naked body, as I slammed the door closed, not giving a damn when I heard one of the paparazzi cry out in pain after he'd stuck his foot in the doorway to prevent me from shutting it.

I flicked the dead bolt, gathered Artie in my arms, and hustled her back to the bed, scooping up clothes as I went. Her shirt went on then her sweats. I yanked my button-down over my arms, did up the buttons, and shoved my legs into my jeans.

And then I sat there.

Wondering what in the fuck I should be doing at that moment.

The knocking started up again, pounding that seemed to reverberate through my clenched teeth. I reached for the room phone and jabbed at the buttons until I got the front desk.

"Why in the fuck are there paparazzi outside of Artemis Miller's door?" I yelled.

"I-I—"

"Call security or the police. I don't give a fuck. Get them out of here." I slammed the receiver down, retrieved my cell from my back pocket. Forty-two missed calls. Text messages from my family, from my assistant, from the studio.

"Fuck," I groaned then sucked in a breath and began dialing. First to my assistant, who thankfully was already in the process of arranging for a driver and security. Next was to the publicist at the studio, who I sent on a mission to stop those pictures from hitting the press. It was illegal in the States to film in someone's private space like they had done, and they shouldn't be allowed to sell the pictures, but I didn't have a whole lot of faith that the photos wouldn't end up somewhere on the internet, considering how low they'd sunk in the first place.

I glanced at Artie, saw she was pale and unmoving. "Hey," I murmured. "It's gonna be okay."

She blinked, blue eyes slowly focusing on me. "Hmm?"

"We'll figure this out," I said. "It'll be fine."

"I—"

My cell buzzed, and I glanced down at its screen then back at Artie. "I—"

"Take it," she murmured, pushing off the bed and crossing over to the desk where her cell was plugged in. "I'm sure I have calls to make."

With a nod, I answered, putting it up to my ear and spending the next few hours putting out fires with the various studios I was working with. I half-expected to get my ass chewed on all fronts, but surprisingly most of the execs were understanding and told me to just keep my head down and keep working, that they'd do their best to get the paparazzi to keep their distance.

But by the time midday rolled around, I knew that I was going to have to face the mob anyway.

The crew would be arriving at the studio in the next few hours and if I was going to make the call time, I would need to leave soon.

Security had arrived and were stationed at the hotel, with one outside Artie's door.

Cars and drivers were ready.

Obviously, it was time to pack up and get out.

My assistant had texted with new hotel information, which I forwarded on to Artie, who'd either been on the phone like me or glued to her laptop, fingers furiously working on the keyboard.

Pocketing my cell, I crossed over to the desk where Artie

was on her computer. What I glimpsed on the screen made my heart sink.

"Fucking hell," I muttered.

The top picture on the gossip site was us from the night before, me pinning Artie against the wall, her legs around my waist, our mouths locked together.

World's Hottest Cougar, was the headline.

She closed the tab, pulled up another. A slightly different angle of the kiss. Another. Her with my mom, both of them smiling at me at the airport. Another. My hand on her ass, but this time the words *exclusive* and *breaking news* topped a longer article.

How anyone's relationship could possibly be breaking news was beyond me, but I'd never understood the fascination with celebrities' personal lives.

Then again, I'd never have considered either Artie or myself celebrities.

She sighed. "This is my fault."

"Bull—"

"Don't finish that *shit*," she muttered and highlighted the name under the final article, a picture of a little old lady next to it, complete with glittering necklaces and poofy white hair.

"Who's Beverly Hawkins?"

"The person I sat next to on the flight over. Fuck, Pierce. I'm so stupid. She was priming me with questions, and I fucking spilled everything about you and me. I opened us up to—"

"Hang on." I placed my hand on her shoulder and squeezed lightly, stopping her as I scanned the article. Once I got to the end, I met her miserable eyes. "So, you're feeling bad because you told a woman you liked me, more than anyone you've ever been with, and that you're falling for me"—I chuckled—"and you're thinking I'll be mad about that?"

Artie brushed my hand away. "This isn't funny!"

"No," I said, tugging her into my arms. "Those photos aren't funny. The guys outside the door aren't acceptable. But, sweetheart, I love you. I don't care if the whole world knows it. That article isn't the problem." I touched her cheek. "In fact, that article is probably the most wonderful thing anyone has ever given me."

Her hair moved wildly as she whipped her head back and forth. "She says I'm a cougar. That I just chew up and spit out men."

"And you said I was different than all the other men."

"I—" She stopped.

"And nowhere in there did they mention a thing about the women *I've* dated. Where's your outrage for that fact? I've dated younger women, and this Beverly woman doesn't mention that? It's bull—"

She kissed me. "No more bullshits," she said against my lips.

"Are you going to freak out?"

"No."

"Promise?"

Her eyes closed then opened, her expression lighter, lips curving. "Okay, fine. I might freak out, but I promise to talk it over with you first."

Relief poured through me. "I'll take it."

She touched my jaw. "You need to go. I probably should keep my distance until we have a little more support."

"I don't think you have to," I said. "But if it makes you more comfortable . . ."

A nod.

"Okay, honey," I said. "We should pack up and head to the next hotel. I'll do that now so I can get to set on time."

"All right."

My cell rang and I reached down to extract it. "Hey, Mom," I said into the receiver.

"Why are there suited men on my doorstep?" she snapped loud enough that Artie winced.

I smiled reassuringly. "In case you've somehow slept through what's plastered everywhere, Artie and I are apparently hitting our celebrity couple status."

"And what does that have to do with them trampling my begonias? They stepped on the grass and—"

I hit mute and kissed the top of Artie's head. "I'll see you later?"

Her eyes were bleak, but almost as quickly as I noticed it, she nodded and stepped back. One more kiss, this time to her lips, and I unmuted long enough to tell my mom I'd replace the begonias.

"They're not replaceable! They're a special variety that . . ."

Off she went.

I hit mute again and headed for the door, uneasy about the look on Artie's face, but knowing she'd need time to process this blow.

"Pierce?" she asked as I reached for the dead bolt.

"Yes, sweetheart?"

"I love you."

My heart skipped a beat, my knees went weak with relief, and my smile was wide enough to hurt my jaw.

"I love you, too." I took a step back toward her, wanting to kiss her, to hold her, to forget about the call time and—

"Pierce? *Pierce?*"

She smiled and nodded at my phone. "I'll talk to you soon."

"Okay, love," I murmured, unmuting my phone and hitting the hallway.

It wasn't until much later that I realized she hadn't promised to see me that evening or meet me at the hotel . . .

Or that soon could mean very different things to different people.

That soon could also mean never.

TWENTY-ONE

Artie

I WAS A COWARD.

I embraced that.

I'd directed my driver to take me to the airport and had called in an old favor to a friend who'd let me borrow her private plane.

"Is this about what's in the news?" Heather O'Keith had asked.

"I need out of Scotland," was all I'd say.

"It's about the news," Heather replied matter-of-factly. "I can get you a plane out of Edinburgh. When will you be there?" We'd taken the next few minutes to discuss details, but before hanging up she had stopped and said, "I feel like it's my duty to ask this next question."

"Heather—" I began.

"No," she said. "I'm speaking as a woman who tried to run from her past, not one that was as tough as yours, but one that still made me feel unworthy and incapable of being in a relationship."

"I'm not . . ." But I couldn't finish the words because I didn't know *what* I was.

I was running. Part of me still felt unworthy.

But it had been different when it was just Pierce and me. A hard pill to swallow, of course, that the paparazzi might be trailing us, but also knowing that he'd been aware of the situation. That while it was something to be adjusted to, it wasn't like his world would implode.

Movie sets were isolated and secure for the most part.

And soon another much juicier celebrity scandal would take top billing over just a director and a producer, even considering my past and our age difference.

It was just . . . begonias.

Or more clearly, Pierce's lovely, perfectly, imperfect family.

Dory had security guards outside her home, trampling her flowers. Soon there would be paparazzi crowded on the street, filming into her house, following her around.

Following Marie and Kate.

Scaring the kids.

And it was the idea of Thomas being frightened by a huge intimidating man with a camera, screaming at him that had done it for me.

It didn't matter if and when this blew over.

I couldn't let my life bleed over into theirs.

"I'm not saying don't take a second and think this through," Heather said, and I knew she understood part of what I was going through. She was in a powerful position, had struggled her way through life and a shitty upbringing to make something of her life. And then that had all almost been unraveled when she'd met Clay Steele.

But they'd figured things out.

They were happily married with a successful joint company.

However, they didn't have the paparazzi hounding them, potentially hurting their families, reporting on every sordid thing from their past.

So, as much as I appreciated her caution and support, I knew she could never get it.

"I've thought it through, Heath."

Silence, then, "Okay."

"I'll call Colin and get you on a plane."

"I owe you one."

"Payment in the form of screeners, as always," she said, voice joking, but I could tell she was worried about me.

I released a breath, forced my tone to be light. "As long as you keep giving me a discount rate on that secure distribution platform, then you've got a deal."

"You're on." A beat. "You'll call, though? If you need a pair of nonjudgmental ears to listen?"

"Yeah." I blinked. "I'll call."

We said goodbye and hung up.

Two hours later I was at the airport.

Thirty minutes after that, we were in the air.

TWENTY-TWO

Pierce

I KNEW something was wrong the moment I went up to my room.

Don't know how I knew, maybe just instinct, maybe it was the way the security guard stationed in the hall outside of Artie's room looked at me, maybe it was just the sinking feeling I'd had all day, growing larger as it twisted and knotted my stomach.

I used the key card to enter my room then dropped my bag onto the desk and used the room phone to call Artie's.

No answer.

My assistant had given me the room number, but it was possible she was wrong.

Though security—

I shook my head and dialed her cell.

No answer.

I texted.

No answer.

I went back out into the hall and knocked on Artie's door.

No answer.

"Haven't seen her come in, sir," the security guard said.

"She's definitely in this room?" I asked.

"I haven't been notified of any changes."

I nodded and went back into my room, dialing my assistant and confirming that Artie had been assigned that room.

"I'll call the front desk," Shelby said. "Make sure the keys were picked up."

"Thanks." I hung up, waffling for a moment before I decided to just do it anyway. I dialed the number for Artie's assistant, Lauren.

"Hello?" she answered.

"It's Pierce."

Her inhale was loud, and it told me enough.

"She's gone," I whispered. "Isn't she?"

"Pierce—" Her voice was sad. "I'm sorry. I don't know. I can't say— I—"

"It's okay."

It wasn't okay. *I* wasn't okay. She'd said she loved me and—

She'd left.

I sank onto the side of the bed and dropped my head in my hands, trying to come up with a plan, with some way to make Artie see reason. But I'd tried. I'd been patient. I'd been understanding. I'd put myself out there and been vulnerable and open. And now I had paparazzi camped outside the hotel, a movie to finish shooting, and . . . my heart had been sliced to pieces.

Exactly as I'd felt the first time Artie had left me.

Almost six years had passed.

And nothing had changed.

TWENTY-THREE

Artie

I GOT ALL the way to the private airfield outside of L.A. before I realized exactly how grievous of an error I'd made.

I'd left Pierce.

I'd left Pierce after promising to always talk it out.

I'd left and—

Just being apart from him like this was absolute agony.

I turned on my cell as I walked to the waiting car, feeling it vibrate and hearing it chime as all of the messages from the last twelve hours came through.

Pierce had texted every hour.

Pierce had called several times.

Pierce had stopped.

That only added to the agony, only added to the idiocy that was me and my brain and my fucking life being ruled for too long by fear. I sank into the back seat, eyes taking a moment to adjust to the light as I wrapped my head around the thoughts in my mind, the feelings in my heart.

Did I want to risk the one thing in my life that had been good?

Did I want to let my past taint it?

But maybe . . . my past would only taint my future if I let it ruin the one good thing I had.

I dropped my head back to the seat and asked the driver to wait.

Then I called Heather.

She answered. "Artie?"

"I fucked—"

"My plane is waiting on the tarmac."

I frowned. "What?"

"You *were* going to finish that statement with *up*, right?"

"Yes?"

"Good," she said. "Colin's crew needs rest before they fly home, but the RoboTech jet is fueled and cleared to leave at terminal two."

"I—" I shook my head. "How'd you know I'd change my mind?"

"Because you're smart. Because you're scared. Because you're strong." Her voice dropped. "But also because you know when it's worth it to take a risk."

"I do?"

"Yes, Artie. You do."

I nodded, repeated without the question mark. "I do."

"You got this," Heather said. "Because you're not stupid enough to let someone as special as Pierce slip from your life without fighting for it."

No question this time. "I do. I do have this."

I hung up, pushed out of the car, and got my ass back onto a plane, trying Pierce's cell once before we took off. It went to voicemail, but I didn't panic.

Pierce Daniels better watch out, because I wasn't ready to give up on us.

I'd finally shed the fear, finally realized what I should be really fighting for.

One way or another, I was going to grovel my way back into his life.

TWENTY-FOUR

Pierce

FOR TWICE IN AS MANY days, pounding on my hotel room door woke me up.

"Motherfucker," I muttered, throwing back the blankets and wondering why in the fuck I was paying for security when they didn't bother to. Stop. The. Assholes. From. Knocking. On. My. Door.

I threw on a T-shirt, glanced at the clock, and huffed in annoyance.

I'd fallen asleep all of thirty minutes before.

And the pounding didn't stop.

I slammed open the dead bolt, scrabbled at the door handle, and yanked the door open. "What the fuck—?"

Blue eyes.

Blond hair.

Pink cheeks.

I didn't think, just reacted, grabbing Artie's arm and tugging her into the room. I slammed the door shut and stared at her for a long moment, eyes searching her for injuries, but knowing I wouldn't find any.

She'd left in fear.

She was back because . . .

I didn't dare to hope.

"Hi, Pierce," she murmured tentatively.

Fuck, that hurt. I whipped around, paced into the room, the nervousness in her tone was fucking agony. We'd made so much progress together and yet, it was right back to this.

"Are you all right?" I asked, facing her.

She shook her head. "No, I'm not." The bleakness in her expression turned my gut.

"Don't worry," I said, shoving a hand through my hair and pacing away again, focusing on the curtains instead of the woman I loved with painful intensity. She'd come here to end things permanently. That was it. That was good, really. She wasn't running anymore. She was talking to me and even if it wasn't what I wanted to hear, I was still proud of her. "I'll finish the film. I'll do the promotion and then I'll leave you alone." I cleared my throat. "The script is yours, if I can't sign over the rights, I'll make sure I'm only a silent partner."

Silence.

I stayed facing the wall. "I'll make this easy on you, Artie. Don't worry. You'll get to make your movies and travel the world. You'll get to have your safety and freedom and not have to worry about me."

More silence.

Fuck. Sighing, I braced myself against the pain of seeing her and spun around.

She had tears on her cheeks.

"It'll be okay, sweetheart."

"No," she said. "It won't. Because the life you just described doesn't have you."

The air froze in my lungs.

She stepped close enough that I could smell her floral scent.

My heart twisted.

"I don't want a life without you, baby. I love you," she said. "I know I failed our first test as a couple. I know I ran when I was supposed to talk. I know I really fucking suck for making you worry for more than twenty-four hours." Her teeth nibbled at her bottom lip. "But I just flew all the way to L.A. and back, and I was equally miserable both ways. You know why?"

I shook my head.

"Because on the first leg I'd known I'd lost you." A beat. "On the second, I worried I wouldn't be able to get you back."

I blinked. "Baby—"

"No," she said. "Let me finish?" I nodded. "I made one promise to you and that was to trust in us, to trust in the friendship we'd built over the years. I promised I wouldn't run, that we would talk things out. And I broke that promise."

"You said that already," I murmured, taking her hands and leading her to the bed. "We're both going to fuck up. I know that, and I don't need you to rake yourself over the coals for it."

She snorted. "And when do *you* fuck up, Pierce?" she snapped. "You're always perfect and—"

"You haven't seen my Lego collection."

Artie blinked. "Um, what?"

"I have an entire room of them—buildings, mini figures, streets, and cars and teeny, tiny food stands. I talk in my sleep, I hog the remote, and I definitely don't eat enough vegetables." I bent a little so our faces were level. "I'm far from perfect, Artie. You've just been so wrapped up in your imperfections that you haven't seen mine."

Her lips parted, a long, slow exhale escaping.

Then her face changed. The torture left her expression, her stiff shoulders relaxed. In turn, I was able to do the same. The fist gripping my gut since the previous evening loosened and my lungs finally began working again.

"I love you," I said. "I don't care if we make the cover on every magazine. I don't care if every reporter starts off an interview with a question about what it's like to be dating the amazingly talented Artemis Miller. I don't care if I need to slow down so that I can make our schedules fit better or take a hundred red-eyes just so we can spend one night together." I cupped her face in my palms. "Because the alternative is that I wouldn't have you. And that's not acceptable."

Her eyes filled with tears, but she blinked them back. "I'm going to screw up."

I grinned. "Ditto."

"I'm not stopping eating pasta even if my ass gets huge and I look horrible in dresses at your premieres."

"Wear pants." I kissed her nose. "And if your ass was bigger, then there would just be more of it for me to grab on to."

She snorted.

I smiled down at the woman I loved, the one who meant so much because she'd come back to me, who'd found the courage to knock on my door at an obscene hour even though she was scared, even though it meant that she'd have to own up to making a mistake.

"You know, it is almost exactly six years to the date that I walked into that restaurant thinking that I was meeting an old, fat, balding guy named Artie."

Her eyes narrowed at me.

"Turned out, the only adjective I got wrong was the fat."

She tackled me to the bed, fingers coming to the outsides of my ribs and digging in. "Pierce Daniels, are you fucking kidding me? Old *and* balding?"

I was laughing too hard to bat her hands away then laughing too hard because she'd actually found a ticklish spot. Eventually,

I got my shit together and captured her wrists, flipping us so her back was on the mattress and I was holding both of them captive in one of mine up and over her head.

She glared.

I dropped a kiss on her lips.

She nipped at mine in response.

And then I was kissing her, our mouths meeting in that perfect collision that was just me and Artie, the heat instantaneous and building, my cock hardening, but more importantly, the feeling of *just right* that was pure Artie, settling back over my heart, seeping into my bones, and reminding me that I was the luckiest son of a bitch on the planet to have a chance with this woman.

It didn't matter that there were years between us.

I didn't care that her past might make our relationship newsworthy.

I didn't care that she might run.

Because I'd go after her.

Always.

Speaking of which, that reminded me. I slowed the kiss, removed my hand that had slid under her shirt, the one that was creeping north to cup those beautiful breasts. I released her wrists and I pushed off.

"What—?"

"I have to make a call real quick."

Shelby answered on the second ring, even though it was late at night in L.A. "Pierce, everything okay?"

"Everything is perfect," I said. "The only thing is that I need you to cancel the plane.

I could feel her smile through the speaker. "Artie came back?"

"I plead the fifth."

That smile had to be morphing into a grin. Or maybe that

was just me. "Artie came back," Shelby said, and this time it was a statement rather than a question. "I'm happy for you, Pierce."

"Thanks." I sucked in a breath. "Rhonda still good to cover for today?"

"I'll confirm and tell her to expect you on set bright and early tomorrow."

"Thanks, Shelb." We exchanged goodbyes and hung up. I tossed the cell on the nightstand and rotated back to face Artie, who had stiffened beneath me, eyes going wide. I just cupped her cheek and shook my head.

"I won't let you run," I murmured. "Not now. Not ever."

No movie would ever be more important than her. No job or interview or location scouting or award.

"You arranged for a plane?"

I nodded. "Good thing it couldn't take off last night because of bad weather, huh?"

Her lips curved and she shook her head. "That would have been a long flight for nothing." She tapped her chin. "Don't know how that feels or anything."

I grinned. "Well, thank you for coming back."

"I—I don't even know what to say to that." Another shake of her head. "I shouldn't have panicked and—"

"No coals, remember?" I brushed my thumb over her bottom lip. "And you don't *need* to say anything. Just stay for now. Be with me for as long as you can and then keep in touch with me when you can't. Send me silly set stories or pretty pictures of where you are when we're apart. Make me jealous when you're eating all that delicious pasta." I brushed back the hair from her face. "You don't need to say the perfect thing or make a grand gesture. I just want you."

She sniffed. "Pierce."

"I know. I'm romantic and say all the right things."

A snort, the tears fading. "Is this where we circle back to you calling me old and balding?"

"Who said either of those were an insult?"

Artie sighed and dropped her head back to the pillow, both of her palms resting on the outsides of my arms. "I love you, Pierce Daniels, even if you can be the most infuriating man on the planet."

I dropped a kiss to her forehead. "See? Not perfect."

She broke out into peals of laughter, her lips curving up as my mouth drifted lower, seeking out hers. I kissed her, that laughter filling me, making mine join in with hers.

It was beautiful.

It was two imperfect people finding their way to . . . *not* perfect.

Just pretty damn right.

And that was perfect to me.

EPILOGUE

Artie, Two years later

"AND HOW DOES it feel to see your wife up there receiving the top award for acting?" the interviewer asked Pierce, who was sitting next to me on one of the most popular daytime talk shows in the country.

I felt like absolute shit.

Neither of us had slept the previous night.

Filled with too much adrenaline, attending too many after parties.

Drinking *way* too much for a person my age.

Cue the internal snort. Forty-four was the new twenty-four as far as I was concerned.

Yeah, sure. But it turned out that the script Pierce had bought two years before had been beyond special, so special, in fact, that we hadn't been able to find the perfect lead.

Until I'd drifted out from behind the camera to help our male lead run his lines prior to a few screen tests.

Until Pierce and I *and* that famous male heartthrob had realized what we'd had.

Lightning in a bottle.

I wasn't sure I'd be able to do it.

But Pierce had been certain. And so . . . more golden statues.

This time for Pierce's directing *and* somehow for my acting, grossly out of shape, but raw and instinctive, and even I had to admit that it had been pretty good.

I didn't recognize my life any longer, couldn't believe the sharp left it had taken, couldn't understand how I'd changed so much in so short a time. But then I turned to the audience and I saw Marie and Kate and Thomas and Dory and Grayson and Hank and *all* the rest of the Daniels crew, and I knew.

It was because of them.

It was because of Pierce.

It was because of me.

I'd opened myself up to the possibility of something, I'd taken a chance, I'd been vulnerable . . . and it had worked.

Because of my family.

Because of my man.

Because of me.

Pierce chuckled at the question, drawing my attention back to him and the interviewer and the fact we were on camera. He knew I'd drifted off, as he always seemed to know everything that was going through my head, and so he laced our fingers together, drawing our hands into his lap.

"How do you think it feels?" he asked, and then his words weren't for the camera or for the audience. They weren't for anyone except for me. "I am so incredibly proud of you," he whispered in my ear as he hugged me tightly.

He didn't take into account the live mic.

He didn't think that the gentle way he cupped my cheek afterward, eyes locked on mine for a long moment would be immortalized in gifs and memes and social media videos talking about the types of boyfriends women dreamed of.

He didn't know we'd go viral for a second time.

But he also didn't give a damn in the least.

And I didn't either.

EPILOGUE
PART TWO

Pierce, Eight Months Later

SO, funny story, it turned out that the reason Artie had felt so awful the morning after our joint Oscar celebration had been because she was pregnant.

Well, that and the obscene amount of wine and pasta we'd consumed the night before.

We'd known that Artie had missed her periods for two months, but when she'd shrugged it off, saying it was probably pre-menopause and that I'd better trade her in for a younger model, I'd put any hope of kids out of my mind.

Would I have liked a child with Artie?

Of course. I loved her. The thought of having a baby with her was exhilarating, not terrifying.

But I also understood that sometimes timing didn't work out and if we got around to not being too busy for a family, then we would look into adoption or surrogacy.

Still, as the days after the awards show went on and the nausea didn't abate, I strong-armed her into going to the doctor.

Who'd strong-armed her into taking a pregnancy test.

Which had come back positive.

And then there had been six months of furious preparation, six months of Artie having every test done possible because she was convinced that the night of celebrating had hurt the baby— even though the obstetrician had assured her that most likely everything was fine—and that her age wouldn't negatively affect the precious life growing inside her.

Though she *was* high-risk, because of her age, and so we did every test, read every book. We prepped and talked to Marie and Kate and—

Now we were here.

With my gorgeous baby girl in my arms and my gorgeous wife asleep after working so hard to give birth to our child.

A beautiful, perfect girl.

Just like her mama.

I stroked a finger down her nose and made the same promise to her as I did to her mother on our wedding day a year before.

"I don't know what our future will bring us, but I do know we'll have hiccups and bumps and sharp turns. I can't promise that we'll have eternity together or that everything will always be easy." I pressed my lips to her forehead. "But I *can* promise that we'll figure it out together. You, your mom, and me."

When I looked up, Artie was smiling at me tiredly.

"Too perfect," she murmured.

"No," I said. "That's you."

I bent, touched my lips to hers, and I held on to my girls.

I might not be able to promise eternity, but I was going to do my damndest to give it to them anyway.

EPILOGUE
PART THREE

Eden

I WALKED out of the hospital after visiting Artie and Pierce's beautiful baby girl, my heart filled with so much joy for my friends.

I owed the director-producer duo a huge debt of gratitude.

They'd cast me in the surprise box office success, *Carrot*, a few years before, and because of that, I'd had my dream of crossing over from model to actress fulfilled. I'd had one of those model urban legends, a pretty girl seen on the street and approached, my career in modeling easy and fruitful. I hadn't been taken in by a creepy old man with a casting couch nor had I been assaulted or belittled or had a diary filled with horror stories like so many of my contemporaries.

I was lucky.

I was empty.

Because I'd been merely a doll to be dressed up and styled in someone else's vision, a simple vessel to be filled with someone else's ideas. I was to be looked at and not looked in—

I snorted. It wasn't like acting was so different. I was still judged by the way I looked, magazines still frequently accused me of being pregnant after I'd had a big lunch, or linked me with any male I was seen exchanging a few words with.

But I wasn't empty any longer.

I felt and lived and finally was *me*.

So much self-contemplation for so early in the morning, but then again, seeing a precious little bundle of life brought so newly into this world would do that to a girl.

I was absolutely thrilled for Artie and Pierce. They were the real deal and deserved every bit of their success—film or family version. Smiling to myself, I reached into my purse for my keys then promptly dropped them to the ground.

Ugh.

I bent—

"I know that ass."

A gasp of outrage on my lips, I straightened and whipped around, ready to tell off the arrogant bastard who'd dared—

Damon Garcia.

Photographer extraordinaire and—

He grinned.

Man who still wanted to get into my pants.

Now, I wasn't a prude. I slept around enough to have been called a whore by more than one publication. It wasn't more than most men in Hollywood, but because I was a woman, it was noticed and frowned upon.

I just couldn't bring myself to care.

I practiced consensual, safe sex.

If we both were attracted to each other and it was safe, then I didn't hesitate to go for what I wanted.

Maybe that made me a whore.

Maybe I didn't care what other people thought about me.

But Damon?

Damon, I didn't sleep with.

Damon, I didn't fuck or kiss or touch.

Because I knew if I allowed myself a taste, I would never have enough.

I was frozen in place when he bent in front of me and picked up my keys, extending them toward me. That was when I made my first mistake. My fingers brushed his as I took them back. Heat exploded up my arm, my stomach went tingly, and my voice was breathy as I asked, "What are you doing here?"

"I live here now. Well, not the hospital—I'm visiting a friend —but here in town." He smiled, and that paired with the news of him being in L.A. hit me hard upside the head. So hard, it knocked my common sense loose and allowed me to make my second mistake.

Because I didn't run after I'd said, "Oh, that's great."

My third came when he asked, "Want to grab a drink tonight and catch up?"

To which I said, "Yes," instead of "Absolutely not."

My fourth?

Well, my fourth came when I finally gave into the draw that was Damon Garcia and woke up naked in my bed beside him.

And then he wouldn't leave.

CLOSE UP

Eden and Damon's story is now available. Get your copy at
www.books2read.com/CloseUpEF

LOVE, CAMERA, ACTION

Did you miss any of the Love, Camera, Action Series books?
Find information about the full series here.
Or keep reading for a sneak peek into each of book 1 below!

Dotted Line
Love, Camera, Action #1
Get your copy at books2read.com/DottedLine

Olivia

THE COLD VOICE hit my spine before I made it to my chair.

"What did you say?"

Cole McTavish.

A tall hunk of a former hockey player, all muscled thighs and towering height, with a face that would have been classified as beautiful if not for the several-times-broken nose, the jagged scar along his jaw, and the small, smooth one bisecting his left eyebrow.

Further that, he was about as opposite from me as anyone I'd ever met.

Relaxed, always ready with an easy smile, Cole never raised his voice—at least *off* the ice. On it, he'd been a terror, a virtually unstoppable force who'd fought when needed and didn't back down from protecting a teammate.

I'd also been his agent while he was playing.

After he'd retired, I'd transitioned him over to Devon, who'd helped him refine his brand for post-playing opportunities. Now, he was the face for a few hockey companies and one well-known corporation that sold watches. Though, to my and the rest of the female populace's dismay, he'd turned down the swimwear ads.

I'd been with him in the locker room enough to know what was under those flannel shirts and jeans.

It was definitely billboard worthy.

Lane started to push by him, but Cole grabbed his shoulder and stepped into my office, forcing Lane back.

Devon Scott trailed them in, a stormy expression on his face.

I glanced at my boss and shook my head, silently telling him I'd already handled it, but Dev shook his head firmly back at me. Which was when I realized that what Lane had said must have been worse than I'd thought. Normally, Devon would never get involved in an argument between my employees and myself unless I asked him to.

Which I didn't.

Since I handled my own shit.

"Tell her what you said."

My gaze flashed to Cole and his darkened face. "It's—"

Emerald eyes locked onto mine, sparking fire. "Tell her," he said, and Lane must have realized exactly how deep of a pile of shit he'd dived into because when I broke Cole's stare to glance at my assistant, his face had gone pale.

I rested my hip against my desk. "I don't need to hear it. Lane, get the file."

Devon crossed his arms. "Tell her," he said. "If you're man enough to mutter it under your breath, you're man enough to say it aloud."

Lane shook off Cole and spun to face me. "Fine," he snapped. "I said that you're such a fucking bitch."

My lips curved and I huffed. "Okay, great, thanks. Now, back to work."

Lane's jaw fell open.

A curl of amusement crept onto Dev's face.

Cole appeared even more infuriated.

Lane somehow went paler. "Wh-what?"

"I've got a ton of work," I told him, "and you say bitch like it's a bad thing." I transferred my gaze to Cole and Dev. "*All* of you are acting like it's the worst insult in the world." I laughed. "Believe me, I've been called worse."

"It's unacceptable," Dev said, and I loved the guy for it.

But this was also the way of the world.

Most men despised strong women. We were told to smile or look happy or be fine with the scraps they tossed our way. If I'd had an issue with men calling me a bitch, I would have quit this male-dominated field ten years ago when I'd been a lowly assistant like Lane and my boss had been a lot worse than a bitch.

But I hadn't.

I'd put my head down, got my shit done.

And I'd learned to not give two craps when a man thought I was a bitch.

Because it had become my anthem.

When I negotiated my client to have equivalent perks in their contract, I was a bitch.

When I demanded a different client have access to the same off-season training as the rest of the team, I was a bitch.

When I secured a bonus that was similar to the rest of the big names on the roster, I was a bitch.

So, fine.

I was a bitch.

Great. Congrats. Moving on.

—Get your copy at www.books2read.com/DottedLine

LOVE, CAMERA, ACTION

Dotted Line

Action Shot

Close Up

End Scene

ALSO BY ELISE FABER

***Billionaire's Club* (all stand alone)**

Bad Night Stand

Bad Breakup

Bad Husband

Bad Hookup

Bad Divorce

Bad Fiancé

Bad Boyfriend

Bad Blind Date

Bad Wedding (July 19th, 2020)

Bad Engagement (October 12th, 2020)

Love, Action, Camera (all stand alone)

Dotted Line

Action Shot

Close-Up

End Scene

***Love After Midnight* (all stand alone)**

Rum and Notes

Virgin Daiquiri

On The Rocks (September 27th, 2020)

***Gold Hockey* (all stand alone)**

Blocked

Backhand

Boarding

Benched

Breakaway

Breakout

Checked

Coasting

Centered

Life Sucks Series **(all stand alone)**

Train Wreck

Hot Mess (coming soon)

Roosevelt Ranch Series **(all stand alone, series complete)**

Disaster at Roosevelt Ranch

Heartbreak at Roosevelt Ranch

Collision at Roosevelt Ranch

Regret at Roosevelt Ranch

Desire at Roosevelt Ranch

Phoenix Series **(read in order)**

Phoenix Rising

Dark Phoenix

Phoenix Freed

Phoenix: LexTal Chronicles **(rereleasing soon, stand alone, Phoenix world)**

From Ashes

In Flames

To Smoke

KTS Series

Fire and Ice (Hurt Anthology, stand alone)

Stand Alones

Someday, Maybe (YA)

ABOUT THE AUTHOR

USA Today bestselling author, Elise Faber, loves chocolate, Star Wars, Harry Potter, and hockey (the order depending on the day and how well her team -- the Sharks! -- are playing). She and her husband also play as much hockey as they can squeeze into their schedules, so much so that their typical date night is spent on the ice. Elise changes her hair color more often than some people change their socks, loves sparkly things, and is the mom to two exuberant boys. She lives in Northern California. Connect with her in her Facebook group, the Fabinators or find more information about her books at www.elisefaber.com.

f facebook.com/elisefaberauthor

a amazon.com/author/elisefaber

BB bookbub.com/profile/elise-faber

O instagram.com/elisefaber

g goodreads.com/elisefaber

P pinterest.com/elisefaberwrite